Bo
ki

Muz... grenade. It hit the ground and broke into multiple skip-chasing bomblets. The three submunitions bounced and skipped in opposite directions borne on their spewing jets of irritant gas.

A curtain of gray smoke covered the entrance of the corral. Guns began firing from all directions. The men were Mafia hitters, and Bolan was depending on that fact. The vast majority of gangsters were assassins, not soldiers. They came to their targets smiling or from behind in dark alleys. A standing gunfight was their last, worst option.

Battle experience and body armor were Bolan's main advantage.

The Executioner raised both pistols and began shooting in earnest.

MACK BOLAN ®
The Executioner

The Don Pendleton's Executioner®

TERMINAL ZONE

A GOLD EAGLE BOOK FROM
WORLDWIDE®

TORONTO • NEW YORK • LONDON
AMSTERDAM • PARIS • SYDNEY • HAMBURG
STOCKHOLM • ATHENS • TOKYO • MILAN
MADRID • WARSAW • BUDAPEST • AUCKLAND

First edition November 2005
ISBN 0-373-64324-1

Special thanks and acknowledgment to
Chuck Rogers for his contribution to this work.

TERMINAL ZONE

Where there is a visible enemy to fight in open combat…many serve, all applaud and the tide of patriotism runs high. But when there is a long, slow struggle, with no immediate visible foe, your choice will seem hard indeed.

—John F. Kennedy 1917–1963
Address to the graduating class,
U.S. Naval Academy, June 6, 1961

Some might view my life as hard. I fight evil where it hides. But I am not seeking glory, only justice. I have no other choice.

—Mack Bolan

THE
MACK BOLAN
LEGEND

Nothing less than a war could have fashioned the destiny of the man called Mack Bolan. Bolan earned the Executioner title in the jungle hell of Vietnam.

But this soldier also wore another name—Sergeant Mercy. He was so tagged because of the compassion he showed to wounded comrades-in-arms and Vietnamese civilians.

Mack Bolan's second tour of duty ended prematurely when he was given emergency leave to return home and bury his family, victims of the Mob. Then he declared a one-man war against the Mafia.

He confronted the Families head-on from coast to coast, and soon a hope of victory began to appear. But Bolan had broken society's every rule. That same society started gunning for this elusive warrior—to no avail.

So Bolan was offered amnesty to work within the system against terrorism. This time, as an employee of Uncle Sam, Bolan became Colonel John Phoenix. With a command center at Stony Man Farm in Virginia, he and his new allies—Able Team and Phoenix Force—waged relentless war on a new adversary: the KGB.

But when his one true love, April Rose, died at the hands of the Soviet terror machine, Bolan severed all ties with Establishment authority.

Now, after a lengthy lone-wolf struggle and much soul-searching, the Executioner has agreed to enter an "arm's-length" alliance with his government once more, reserving the right to pursue personal missions in his Everlasting War.

Prologue

The nurse on duty screamed as the man shambled into emergency. The man had no skin. He was a purple mass of muscles and veins that were sloughing off his bones. He was naked save for a dress shirt drenched in blood that made his nudity even more lurid. Pink-tinged bodily fluids seeped from every inch of his body that was not openly bleeding. Bloodstained teeth chattered between the remaining shreds of lips. He reeled forward like a broken marionette, hacking and gurgling into the ward.

A doctor rushing through the emergency room screamed in horror as he ran right into the man. He flailed as the man seized him by the shoulders, the purplish-black flesh of his fingertips smearing the doctor's smock. The doctor fell to the floor with the horror on top of him, the two of them locked in a horrific embrace. The man let out a horrible moan, his tongue lolling from between blackened gums like the pulverized arm of an octopus.

The admitting nurse stabbed her finger on the intercom. Her voice rose to a panicked shriek. "Dr. Strong! Paging Dr. Strong! Dr. Strong to Emergency immediately!"

"Dr. Strong" was hospital slang for sending the largest and most powerful orderlies to restrain a violent patient. The nurse's hand shook as she punched in the code for the police. The operator picked up and asked her what the nature of the emergency was. All the nurse could do was scream as the moaning thing on top of the doctor disgorged about a half a gallon of vibrant liquid.

A blonde built like a fullback and a Métis the size of a refrigerator burst through the emergency-room doors. The orderlies were expecting a drug addict on a bad jag or a mental patient who had neglected his medications. They both skidded to a halt at the sight of the abomination struggling with the doctor.

The blonde's jaw worked up and down. "Oh Jesus…oh Jesus…oh Jesus…" He started to step forward, but his partner's huge hand clamped down on his shoulder.

"Todd, don't go near him. Go around him. Go to the door and lock it." The Métis orderly turned to the nurse. "Jeannie, call security, have them block all the entrances. No one comes in. No one goes out."

The police dispatcher was asking in ever-louder tones for Jeannie to calm down and describe her situation exactly.

"Right…Jimmy…you're right." The admitting nurse began to try to describe the situation on the floor.

The man on the floor was weakening; he appeared to be bleeding out. The doctor flailed and wiped hysterically at the blood and jellied fluids all over his chest and face.

Dr. Shelly Brooke was the head of emergency for the evening. She stepped into the lobby with a syringe of Thorazine ready. "What the hell is going on?"

Her jaw dropped at what he saw.

Jimmy pointed at the thing collapsed on top of Dr.

Finch. "That walked in a minute ago. Todd and me? We ain't touching it. We ain't touching Finch, neither."

"No." Dr. Brooke nodded slowly without looking away from the collapsed man on top of Dr. Finch. "Don't touch either one of them." She turned to the admitting desk. "Jeannie, tell the police we have an infectious disease emergency at the hospital. Tell them to set up barricades around the hospital and quarantine the area."

"Right…" Jeannie's voice shook as she relayed Dr. Brooke's orders.

Dr. Brooke went behind the counter and pulled out a binder. She flipped through it until she found the number for the Centers for Disease Control in Atlanta. There was a long list of numbers. She chose the one in bold red letters.

She punched the number into the telephone.

The line answered partway through first ring. "This is the CDC Biological Outbreak emergency line. Please state your name, exact location and situation."

"My name is Dr. Shelly Brooke, St. Clare's Hospital, the city of St. John's, Newfoundland, Canada. I have a biological outbreak situation. Local police have been informed and the hospital is being quarantined." Dr. Brooke's voice sank as she watched the man bleed out. Dr. Finch had fainted dead away. "Pathogen and vector…unknown."

1

Quebec

"Well, at least we know it works." The Moor slid the newspaper onto his boss's desk. The Boss lit a cigarette and gazed out the window at the St. Lawrence River. He was a big man in an immaculately tailored French-cut business suit. He had a rather disturbing resemblance to the actor Leonardo DeCaprio if the movie star had let himself go to seed, gained fifty pounds, and now made a living beating people to death on the waterfront with his fists. The Boss turned his attention to the newspaper on his desk. The headline of *Le Soleil* consisted of a single French word. It took up a quarter of the page: PESTE!

Plague.

Beneath it was the French headline Newfoundland: The Rock Under Quarantine.

The news media was filling the airwaves with lurid descriptions of a hideous disease. There were only seven known cases, but the horror of the symptoms had thrown fears of an epidemic out of all proportion. Panic was setting in and the Royal Canadian Mounted Police had been mobilized to patrol St. John's.

The Boss blew a smoke ring and nodded to himself. The Moor was right.

It had worked—like a charm.

"How many of the victims are ours?" he asked.

"That we know of, three." The Moor scowled. "One is Phillipe, he's the one who staggered into the hospital and started this mess. Phillipe's dead. The other two are Sylvan and George. They are still alive and in the hospital. Their infection is in an advanced state, and they are in critical condition. Drastic steps are being taken to save them. The other four currently known cases are people Sylvan and George came in contact with but have no connection to us."

"Sylvan and George are fucked, but if their tongues haven't rotted out of their mouths yet, they might be able to scream something important." The Boss stubbed out his cigarette angrily. "I want the situation taken care of."

"I would send Carlo, but entry points to the island are being controlled by the military. It will be very risky to try to get any of our own people inside. I fear we will have to rely on the local pool of talent." The Moor frowned at the thought of what the local talent on Newfoundland was likely to consist of.

"Make it happen." The Boss stared out at the gleaming river again. "I believe that leaves two of our boys still missing."

"Yes, the Prettys twins. Sylvan's cousins, Baron and Ames. They have relatives outside of the capital. Someplace around Trinity Bay, I believe. Finding them should not be difficult."

"Go ahead with the locals. We can't afford to wait, but I want Carlo on the Rock. I want him to find a way onto the island within twenty-four hours. I want him on-site to tie up any loose ends."

Both men smiled. They knew those loose ends were most likely going to be the local talent once they had finished their job. Carlo was the most ruthless man either of them had met in a lifetime of brutal criminal behavior. In the dark world of organized crime, Carlo was the bump in the night that even the hardest of the hard men feared.

"Well, if there is one man who can sneak through a military blockade, it's Carlo. And one man should be easier to insert than a team. He prefers to work alone, anyway," The Moor said.

"Good. I want Sylvan and George dead by dawn. I want the Prettys brothers found and killed within forty-eight hours. Make it happen," The Boss said as he lit himself another cigarette. "It is time to move on to the next phase."

Newfoundland

IT WAS ONE OF THE WORST things Mack Bolan had ever seen. He had seen firsthand the effects of leprosy and Ebola, and been forced to look upon the worst horrors that war machines and the sickest criminal imaginations could inflict upon the human body. But the man behind the plastic containment curtain took the prize. "He walked into the hospital in that condition?"

"Yes." Dr. Nikos Ferentinos sighed at the state of the corpse. "What looks like postmortem decomposition was actually taking place while the subject was still alive. Apparently he still retained at least rudimentary rational thought processes and motor capability. It's absolutely extraordinary." He scratched his short beard and eyed Bolan quizzically. "Pardon me, but just who are you again?"

The Executioner ignored the question as he regarded the body on the gurney. The quarantine area had been isolated in the basement of the hospital. A Canadian army chemical warfare tent had been set up in the cavernous interior. A pair of servicemen in full chemical biological warfare gear and carrying rifles guarded the door. Inside the enclosure, oxygen tents acted as makeshift containment rooms. Three of the oxygen tents were occupied by the living. The victims had been given dangerously large batteries of drugs, all of which so far had been of no avail. Bolan gazed across the tent as surgeons and nurses operated through plastic sleeves in the tents. For the moment, the best the doctors could do was cut out all infected areas of the body. The two advanced patients had undergone multiple amputations and massive tissue removal surgeries. Their prognosis for survival was very low as fresh outbreaks were detected in their bodies on an hourly basis. Even if they lived, they would spend the rest of their lives in hospital.

Dr. Finch appeared to be lucky. The surgeons had removed the upper dermal layer of his face and neck, and his condition was stable. It was possible that with repeated skin grafts he might look human again, eventually.

There was only one saving grace to the pathogen. The doctors were cautiously optimistic that it was transmitted through physical contact rather than being airborne.

"So," Dr. Ferentinos continued, frowning, "just what is your epidemiological experience, Doctor?"

Bolan thought about the horrors he had seen in his life. "I had Ebola once," he said.

Ferentinos's jaw dropped. "Jesus."

Bolan's gazed stayed on the corpse. "So who is he?" he asked, ignoring the doctor's look of disbelief.

"We're not sure yet. There is nothing left of the dermis to take a fingerprint from. We have ID on the other two, and the police are looking for any connections between them. However, since his state is the most advanced and no other cases have been reported in the last twenty-four hours, for the moment we are assuming our friend here is our primary vector. We're waiting on a special RCMP forensics team to come and obtain a dental impression from the subject. Luckily, whatever the pathogen is, it doesn't appear to attack the bone or dental structures of the body."

Bolan nodded at the gurney and its contents. "It's a flesh-eater."

"Well, yes. In a manner of speaking." Dr. Ferentinos grimaced. But that's not a term I like to use."

"You'd prefer Group A Streptococcal Bacteria," Bolan stated.

"You know, the term 'flesh-eating epidemic' has a way of starting a panic in the general population." The doctor regarded Bolan dryly. "You may have already observed it took a thousand Mounties in full dress uniform to calm things down on this island. This is Canada. We're not exactly used to the idea of seeing the RCMP patrolling the streets with machine guns and military helicopters orbiting in our skies. We don't like it, and there are already rumors that this is a situation that came to us courtesy of our friend and ally south of the border."

Ferentinos's weary smile went positively sardonic. "But I suspect that you're here to give me every assurance that it didn't."

"I can't assure you of anything, Doctor. That's not my job."

Ferentinos blinked. "You know, I've been told to offer you every courtesy and assistance, but I still have no goddamn idea who you are."

"I've been told you're the best in your field and that I can rely on you with the security of your nation and mine," Bolan countered.

Dr. Ferentinos smiled at the compliment, but his eyes hardened. "You know flattery will get you everywhere, but—"

"Let's step outside and talk," Bolan said.

They stepped out of the tent as the other doctors inside struggled to save the stricken men's lives.

Bolan's head snapped up immediately. His nose wrinkled as he scented the air.

Ferentinos frowned. "What is it?"

The Executioner's eyes went to slits. The elevator door was open. Six men in orderly uniforms were pushing a wheeled cart heavily laden with oxygen cylinders and boxes of medical supplies. One of them was showing a clipboard to the guard.

"You smell that?" Bolan asked.

Dr. Ferentinos sniffed the air. "Well I don't know, I—" His brow furrowed. "Smells like someone's been smoking."

Bolan could see a crushed-out butt oozing smoke on the elevator floor.

"Dr. Ferentinos, this is Canada and I'm an American. We have some fairly draconian antismoking laws in the U.S., but this is a hospital under quarantine and you and I are in a containment area. Is smoking allowed?"

"No, the entire hospital is nonsmoking."

"We're about to get hit," Bolan said as he blurred into motion.

"Hit? What do you mean..." Dr. Ferentinos's eyes went wide as a Beretta 93-R pistol appeared in Bolan's hand like a magic trick.

The 9 mm weapon had been converted to .22 caliber. A stubby black suppressor cylinder had been mated to the muzzle, and the highly modified magazine held fifty rounds rather than the usual twenty. What the pistol lacked in power it made up for in silence and tack-driving accuracy, and, its .22-caliber projectiles could be sent forth in bursts of three.

It was one of Bolan's "sensitive situation" weapons.

Bolan's voice boomed in the echo chamber of the basement. He extended his weapon and shouted, "Freeze!"

"What the fuck are you doing?" The soldier stationed outside the tent entrance stared at Bolan in shock as he struggled to unsling his rifle.

The orderlies by the elevator didn't stop. Instead they swore and began reaching forward. The 93-R cycled in Bolan's hand. An orderly reaching into a box jerked as the 3-round burst blossomed into bloodstains across the chest of his blue smock. The man fell against the elevator door frame. His hands came out of the box dragging the ugly, black, compact shape of a submachine gun. Bolan put a second burst into his skull, and the would-be assassin collapsed to the floor.

The heads of the guards by the elevator whipped back and forth in confusion as they went for their weapons.

Automatic weapon fire erupted like thunder. One of the guards was shredded as he tried to unlimber his rifle. Bolan dropped another orderly. The second guard was smarter. He ignored his rifle and slapped leather for his pistol. Bolan brought down three more of the orderlies, but he could not save the second guard. The soldier had barely cleared his holster when the top of his head came apart from a point-blank burst.

Assassins began spilling out of the elevator, spraying their weapons like fire hoses.

The guard beside Ferentinos staggered and fell as bullets walked up his chest.

"Down!" Bolan dived behind a pile of supply crates and dragged the doctor with him. "Crawl! Into the tent! Get the doctors and nurses into the back of the basement!"

The doctor nodded.

"Can you shoot?" Bolan asked.

"Yes! I mean no! I was duck hunting…once. I didn't hit shit."

Bolan hooked the dead guard's rifle. He flicked off the safety and shoved the rifle into the doctor's hands. "Hit something," he said as he stripped the fallen soldier of his pistol.

Ferentinos body-blocked a doctor coming out of the tent to see what was happening. People inside the containment tent were screaming in fear and confusion. Half a dozen automatic weapons began spraying indiscriminately through the military green plastic wall of the containment tent.

Bolan rose with pistol in each hand. The Canadian military issue 9 mm Browning Hi-Power barked in his right hand. Its report drowned out the slight sound of the machine pistol in his left. Both weapons blazed. The enemy was coming forward, pushing their cart ahead of them as cover.

The assassins had proved themselves amateurs. They had smoked on their way down to the basement. They were not wearing body armor and they were using a cart laden with oxygen tanks as cover.

The Executioner dropped his aim and emptied the Browning into the pyramid of oxygen cylinders as fast as he could pull the trigger. He jerked as he took a burst in the stomach and staggered as another hit him in chest. The Kevlar of his soft body armor held.

Blue flame suddenly squirted out of an oxygen cylinder in a high-pressure jet, shrieking like a teakettle on steroids. The man whose face was blasted by the flame fell back blistering and screaming. Bolan had blasted eleven holes in the cylinders, and they ignited into streamers of fire.

Bolan threw himself behind the crates.

The cylinders did not technically explode, but the high-pressure tanks ruptured and burst with considerable violence, sending ragged chunks of aluminum shredding through the assassins.

Within half a heartbeat of the tanks bursting, more than twenty thousand liters of pure oxygen ignited. The cart and the assassins diving for cover behind it were enveloped in the expanding ball of fire. Blistering heat washed over Bolan. His cover of stacked medical equipment fell on top of him in an avalanche of overpressure. The plastic wall of the containment tent behind him blackened and bubbled.

A man rose up from beneath the cart, miraculously unscathed by the fireball. He looked at Bolan with pure hatred. The Browning in Bolan's right hand was empty. His left hand and the machine pistol it held were entangled in a folding gurney and pinned down by fallen crates. Bolan struggled to free his hand.

A blond man appeared suddenly in the doorway of the stairs. He was of medium-build and wearing a black leather jacket. He held a pistol in his hand. He surveyed the scene for one second and jerked his head at the lone assassin by the cart. "Nico! Finish him!"

Nico stalked forward. He ejected the spent magazine of his machine gun and slammed in a fresh one.

"Hey!" The charred tent flap flew open. Dr. Ferentinos brought his rifle to his shoulder. "Hold it!" he shouted.

Nico rammed the bolt forward on his weapon and aimed it at the doctor.

Ferentinos grit his teeth and pulled the trigger. The rifle was set on full-auto, and the range was only ten yards. He burned twenty rounds into the assassin before he could take his finger off the trigger. Then he awkwardly swung his sights on the man in the stairwell.

Bolan extricated his arm and raised his weapon.

The blond man pointed his pistol. Bullets from Ferentinos's rifle sparked and ricocheted against the door frame, but the assassin took an extra split second to aim. The killer's pistol spit fire. The doctor's hands clenched on his rifle and his remaining rounds sprayed off target striking sparks off of the concrete ceiling as he fell.

Bolan touched off three rapid bursts from his machine pistol, but the killer had already slammed the door. His bullets broke apart in vain against the steel security door. Bolan stopped firing and dropped down beside the doctor. The bullet had pierced Ferentinos squarely through the shoulder, entering and exiting cleanly. The wound was just under the left collarbone and uncomfortably close to the heart. It was an excellent shot at thirty yards, particularly while staring down the barrel of a blazing automatic rifle. The soldier made a note of it.

The men who had come down the elevator were amateurs. The man who had appeared on the stairs was not.

Bolan ripped open a box of medical dressings and bound the doctor's entry and exit wounds. "You all right?"

Ferentinos shook with adrenaline reaction and shock. "I...hit something."

"Yeah, you did," Bolan said. "Thanks."

The elevator doors hissed shut, and the elevator pinged as it began to ascend.

A nurse stuck her head out of the charred tent. She stared wide-eyed at the surrounding carnage. "Are you all right?"

Bolan nodded and glanced back at the beleaguered containment tent. "How are the people inside?"

"Two of the doctors and one of the nurses got hit with stray bullets. One was a head wound but we have them all stabilized. One of our patients flat-lined when his surgery was interrupted. We weren't able to revive him."

Bolan took Ferentinos's uninjured arm. "Help me get him on a gurney. He's bleeding from both sides."

"Right, I'll—"

The elevator doors suddenly opened and RCMP officers poured out waving pistols, shotguns and submachine guns.

Bolan opened his hand and let the 93-R fall. Dr. Ferentinos raised his head. "Nurse, do not sedate me," he said.

The nurse blinked. "Why?"

Ferentinos looked at Bolan. "I want to hear his explanation for all this."

The Mounties fanned out, securing the basement and surrounding them.

Ferentinos smiled wanly. "This is going to be good."

2

Bolan was surrounded by Royal Canadian Mounted Police. Ferentinos sat beside Bolan with his arm in a sling. He looked pale, but he was smiling at Bolan expectantly.

There were ten RCMP officers in the room and their expressions conveyed hostile curiosity. The deputy commissioner of the Atlantic region stared at Bolan as if he were some breed of animal that he could not place. "Mr. Cooper?"

"Matt Cooper," Bolan acknowledged.

The deputy commissioner scanned the file in front of him. "It seems you engaged in a pitched gun battle in the biological containment area of a hospital under quarantine."

"Commissioner," Dr. Ferentinos said, then cleared his throat, "before this line of inquiry goes any further, I would like to point out that Mr. Cooper is responsible for saving the lives of myself and my entire staff."

Bolan duly noted the doctor's support.

"Yes, well…" The commissioner stared down at the file again, frowning.

Bolan smiled benignly. "You seem to have a file on my situation. May I ask what it says?"

"Your file consists of a pair of letters from the Ministers of Justice and National Defence." The commissioner's brow furrowed. "Both of which say I am to show you all professional courtesies and aid you in whatever way I can, within reason. If for any reason I do not deem it wise to assist you, or feel that your activities are not in accordance with Canadian sovereignty or threaten national security, I am to consult with the ministers directly before taking any action."

Bolan could sympathize. The commissioner had a deadly epidemic on his hands and an entire province on the edge of panic. It was his job to keep a lid on things, and now he found himself in a classic, black operations "mushroom situation."

He was being kept in the dark and being fed only shit.

"Mr. Cooper, neither myself, my staff nor my officers appreciate the CIA coming in here and—"

"I don't work for the Central Intelligence Agency," Bolan said.

"Fine." The commissioner shrugged in irritation. "The FBI, NSA, whatever agency you work for, you can't just—"

"I don't work for the United States government."

The commissioner's mouth opened and then closed again. He had no prepared response. "You...don't...work for the United States government?"

"I have a working relationship with it."

"Mr. Cooper, I am not entirely sure I understand what that means," the deputy commissioner said.

"With all due respect, Commissioner, it means you should refer to the letters you received from the Ministers of Justice and National Defence."

The officer made a face like he was being forced to eat

something that violently disagreed with him. He spoke through clenched teeth. "Yes."

"Commissioner, the Royal Canadian Mounted Police is one of the most respected law enforcement agencies in the world. I do not represent an attempt by the United States to take over your investigation here in Newfoundland. The fact is I am in much greater need of your assistance than you are of mine. Despite what those letters say, I am not demanding your assistance. I'm begging you for it."

Bolan gave the commissioner his most winning smile.

The assembled Mounties shifted from foot to foot and looked back and forth between their commanding officer and the big American.

The commissioner cleared his throat. "Perhaps it would be helpful if you could share some information with us."

Bolan chose his words carefully. "I believe we are dealing with a case of germ warfare."

The Commissioner's eyes bugged. "Jesus."

Ferentinos paled.

"Our mystery bacteria may have been weaponized. In a lab. You've asked me what my experience is in these matters. I'm not a physician or an epidemiologist. My experience is in dealing with the kind of people who would do such a thing. We need to find them, now, and deal with them."

Quebec

"HE WAS GOOD."

The Boss was mildly surprised by Carlo's tone over the secure phone. Carlo never said anyone was good.

"Perhaps the opposition was not up to par?"

"Normally, I would agree with you. I wouldn't trust

part-time Newfie leg-breakers with anything beyond being sent out for sandwiches," Carlo said, clearly disgusted. "But they had overwhelming numbers, overwhelming fire-power and had achieved total surprise. One man and a doc-tor with a borrowed army rifle slaughtered the lot of them."

"You don't believe this mystery man was Canadian Special Forces or RCMP?"

"No. He had a suppressed machine pistol. No Cana-dian military or civil authorities carry such weapons."

"Action Direct?"

"No. If French intelligence were on to us, we'd have known it through our own contacts long in advance. This asshole fought with a pistol in each hand like a goddamn cowboy. He stinks like some kind of paramilitary. Frankly, he stinks like an American."

"What do you have on him?"

"Our spies in the RCMP can only tell us that his name is Matt Cooper, which is probably an alias."

"Matt Cooper." The Boss snorted disgustedly. "He even sounds like a cowboy."

"Yes." Carlo's voice was cautionary. "And it would be best to remember he shoots like one, too."

"I thought you said he blew up our men?"

"Yes, he did, and it occurred to him to deliberately shoot the oxygen cylinders, as well."

"You don't think it was an accident?"

Carlo was silent for a moment. "I do not believe this man does anything by accident, and one might surmise that no accident brought him to Newfoundland."

"Very well, then. What was a fucking American paramilitary commando doing in the containment area at St. Clare's?"

"That is a very good question," Carlo conceded.

"I want him dead."

"That would be prudent."

"What is your current situation? Do you have guns?"

"I have all the guns and equipment I need. It is decent men that are required to finish this job."

"Trying to sneak our own soldiers through the quarantine would be perilous. You are going to have to continue to make do with the local talent."

Carlo's silence spoke volumes as to what he thought of using Newfoundland hit men. "Very well. There is other news. Sylvan died during the attack. His surgery was interrupted when his doctor was hit by a stray bullet."

"I heard. What of George?"

"George died this morning. They dressed him like a side of beef and still couldn't save him."

"So the situation is contained."

"The situation at St. Clare's is contained. The Prettys brothers remain at large. I believe they should be our first priority. The RCMP does not realize they are a lead yet. They must be killed before they become one. Once they are taken care of, we can pick off this American at our leisure."

"Do it."

"I have done some investigating and have some ideas where the Prettys may be holing up. I've assembled a team of local talent. A few of them know the area where we are going. However, I do not like the idea of leaving the American unattended, and I do not trust proper surveillance to the locals."

"I can't send a team." The Boss lit a cigarette. "But as you have proved, the quarantine is permeable. I will send the Moor."

3

St. John's was a fishing town and the oldest city in North America. Newfoundland's provincial capital rose up from the waterfront in a series of terraces connected by a dizzying array of stairs and footbridges that led to narrow, winding streets lined with multicolored clapboard houses. It was a very easy place to get lost in. Bolan had deliberately thrown himself into the thick of the maze near the waterfront to see who might try to follow.

The waterfront was famous to tourists for its large number of drinking establishments. But Remy's was not a nice bar. The paint outside was peeling off the walls, and there did not appear to be any paint on the inside. Some rusted whaling equipment and a fishing net had been hung up on the walls haphazardly, and aged sawdust and peanut shells formed patches of mulch on the floor. It was a place only hardened regulars would feel welcome. Most newcomers would turn tail before the door had a chance to swing closed behind them. About twenty patrons lined the bar and filled the rickety tables. The sun was going down, and they had begun their drinking in earnest.

Bolan's presence drew sullen stares but little else.

The soldier sat down at the bar. He watched the reflection of the patrons in the cracked mirror and confirmed his suspicions. He had picked up more than one tail before ducking into Remy's. He motioned the bartender for two shots.

He decided to go with the hot babe first.

The Executioner scooped up the two shots and walked across the room.

The woman had attracted a great deal of attention. Women that good-looking probably didn't enter Remy's often, if it all, and if they did they were slumming or looking to score drugs. The locals tried to drink up enough courage to make their approach. She wore faded jeans with holes ripped in the knees and a baggy, men's sweatshirt that failed to conceal that there was one hell of a figure underneath. Her collar-length strawberry blond hair was pulled back by a frayed pink scrunchie and covered by a Montreal Canadians billed hat.

The faded drapery could not disguise the fact that she did not belong there. Bolan observed that Remy's women sported garish makeup and had press-on painted claws. This woman's nails were cut short and lacquered clear for business. She was wearing hardly any makeup at all, and she didn't need to. Her posture was perfect, and she hadn't touched her beer in five minutes. Bolan was certain that she had been following him in the business district twenty minutes earlier, wearing a well-tailored pantsuit, sunglasses and a black wig. She'd handed him off to a guy dressed like a bum near the waterfront. The bum had shadowed him until Bolan had ducked into Remy's. The woman had to have switched disguises and followed him in.

Bolan suspected the bum was in the alley outside waiting to see if he came out the back.

The Executioner took a seat at her table and noted the glares of the locals. "Hi."

She looked him up and down wearily. "Fuck off."

Bolan shoved the shot toward her. "Cheers."

She looked him in the eyes, picked up the glass and swallowed the whiskey as if she had been nursed on it. "Thanks. Now fuck off," she said with a slight smile.

Her act wasn't bad, and she had the Newfoundland accent down as far as Bolan could tell.

"Are you and the bum my only official tails at the moment?" Bolan asked, then drank his shot. "Because if not, you've got competition."

The woman's face froze. She rolled her eyes as she realized she'd given the game away and sighed in defeat. "I'm impressed," she said quietly.

"You're RCMP?"

"Yeah." The woman took off the cap and shook out her hair. "Sergeant Daniela Antonetti."

"Mind if I see some ID?"

She reached into her purse and then slid her hands across the table.

Bolan took her hands in his. In her palm was a badge. He frowned slightly as he released her. "V Division?"

The woman quickly made the badge disappear. "Territory of Nunavut."

"Nunavut?" The territory of Nunavut was as large as Alaska and California combined. The population topped out at around thirty thousand souls. More than half of the territory was above the Arctic Circle, and the winter lasted nine months. "Could you get any farther north?"

"I'm just a poor girl from Kugluktuk doing the best she can." The Mountie shrugged. "There's always Greenland."

"What're you doing here?"

"I was in Montreal for some administrative training. My superior wants me to take the inspector's exam next year. When the emergency began, all available officers came to the Rock to help restore order. I was doing street duty in full dress uniform. After your scene in the basement of St. Clare's, my superiors decided you needed to be watched until a decision was made on your status. I was off-duty at headquarters when you walked out. They sent me and two other officers to keep an eye on you."

"I thought I was getting my official liaison officer tomorrow," Bolan said.

"Yeah, well, I was supposed to be your unofficial babysitter for tonight. So much for that."

"I'm sure you have other redeeming characteristics."

"Buddy, if I were tracking you across the tundra, you'd already be hog-tied on the back of my horse." Her smile faded. "Who's the other tail?"

"Those two at the table by the front door and the guy by himself at the table next to them. Then there's the two at the table by the back. I believe they're all together. You recognize any of them?"

Antonetti turned in her chair and motioned at the bartender for more shots. As she did, she took in the whole room and turned back to Bolan. "No, but they look local. You sure they followed you?"

"The one by himself, definitely. I made him outside. He came in alone, made a call on his cell phone and a few minutes later his two friends, the little guy and the big guy, showed up. The waitress recognized them, but her body language says they scare her. I think you're right. They're local, and they're local trouble. The two at the back came in a few minutes later. They were subtle, but they called the guys at the table across the room on their cell phones."

"You don't miss much." The Mountie shrugged. "So why do they need five men to watch you?"

"They don't."

"Ah." Antonetti nodded. "They're going to beat the bejesus out of you."

"Actually, cripple or accidentally kill in a barroom brawl is more likely."

The lone waitress arrived and slopped whiskey into their glasses.

"Leave the bottle," Bolan said.

The waitress looked around the seedy bar and shook her head. "We don't leave the bottle."

Bolan slid a fifty onto the table and smiled. "May we please have the bottle?"

A hint of amusement ghosted across the waitress's face. "It's the magic fuckin' word." She palmed the fifty and put a wiggle in her walk for Bolan's benefit as she returned to the bar without the bottle.

Antonetti pretended to sip her drink. "You are a charmer, aren't you?" She put the drink back on the table. "You want me to arrest them?"

"They haven't done anything yet."

"Well, the province is in a state of emergency and St. John's is under martial law. I'm sure I can come up with something," she said quietly. "Listen, you and I are having a grand old time, but I'm still your babysitter. You are not skinning that fancy smoke wagon of yours in here, you read me? If the situation warrants it, I can have a dozen of my boys and twice that in local law here in minutes."

"Skin that fancy smoke wagon?" Bolan grinned. "You are a northern girl, aren't you."

Antonetti's attention focused somewhere behind Bolan. "Here they come, Sunshine."

"Tell you what. Let me play it by ear. Don't identify yourself unless you have to. Jump in if you feel motivated."

A voice boomed by the door. "Hey!"

Bolan nodded as the noose tightened. "Show time."

The big man by the door had half risen from his chair. He was six foot six with a chin like a steam shovel. His blond hair fell to his shoulders, and he had a short beard and mustache. With a sledgehammer and a horned helmet, he could have passed for the Viking God of Thunder in buffalo plaid.

The man made a show of glaring at Bolan. "What the hell are you staring at?"

The waitress cringed. 'Now, Thor—"

Thor.

Bolan almost laughed.

Thor turned blue eyes as pale as murder on the waitress. "Doreen…"

The waitress bolted for the ladies' room. Remy's went

quiet as the patrons watched the proceedings with hushed expectancy. It seemed to be a show they had seen before. The bartender ran a rag over a pitcher. Apparently this was not a cause for concern.

Thor stepped away from the table, grinning unpleasantly. "Get a load of this guy, Leo."

A lean, rat-faced man in matching denim pants and jacket stood at Thor's side. He stared at Bolan and Antonetti with genuine malevolence. Thor was full of his own power. This guy was another matter entirely. He had little man's disease and lived in Thor's shadow. Hurting people was his way of treating the symptoms. Thor was brutal. Bolan knew the little man would be vicious.

Antonetti spoke quietly. "The two in back are standing up."

"I know." The backup was ready if Bolan presented any unexpected problems. But the man at the table by himself made no move to get up. He was midsized and wore a cut blue suit and sunglasses. He sat like he owned the place. Bolan pegged him as the director of the evening's festivities.

Bolan stood.

Thor grinned. "Lord, thunderin' Jesus." He was putting on a show, but his eyes were clear and hard. "If this fuck ain't as ugly as a bucket o' smashed assholes."

The patrons of Remy's laughed unpleasantly.

Antonetti tried turning on the charm. "Now, boys, let's—"

"Shut your gob," Leo snarled.

The girl from Kugluktuk stopped smiling.

"She's cute," Thor said. He grinned at Bolan. "And that's gonna cost you."

"Oh, yeah," Leo agreed. The little man's eyes shone. He poked Bolan in the chest with his finger. Leo was going to instigate, and the minute the soldier moved Thor was going to rain on him like his Norse God namesake. The finger poked again. "Gonna cost you big, motherfu—"

Bolan caught Leo's finger and broke it.

Leo's eyes flared wide in shock.

He held on to Leo's finger and yanked his face into his fist. Leo's head snapped back, his eyes glazing. Bolan yanked on the broken digit again and pulled the thug's arm straight. He slapped his hand up against the back of Leo's elbow and the joint popped as it hyperextended and dislocated.

Leo's eyes went pinpoint bright with awareness, and he let out a thin, high scream. He sagged to the floor, shrieking as Bolan let go.

Remy's patrons gasped in collective shock.

Thor stared. The entire action had taken less than three heartbeats. Thor's pale eyes met Bolan's, and for a split second the big man showed doubt.

"For fuck's sake!" The suit at the table shouted angrily. "Get him!"

Thor lunged, his huge hands shooting out for Bolan's throat.

The Executioner dropped to one knee. He put all of his two hundred plus pounds into his right fist and buried it two inches beneath Thor's belt buckle.

Thor sagged over Bolan's shoulder.

"Behind you!" Antonetti shouted.

Bolan heard the footsteps. He stood, heaving Thor across his shoulders in a fireman's carry and flung him into the two men charging from behind.

One man fell, the other man staggered. The standing man reached into his pocket and came out with a lead-loaded sap. Antonetti rose from her chair. Her body torqued as she drove the knife-edge of her hand into the side of the man's neck from behind.

The sap man dropped as if he'd been shot.

"Knife!" Antonetti shouted.

Bolan had heard the metallic click behind him and was already on it.

Leo was up. His dislocated arm dangled at his side. He lunged with the switchblade glittering in his hand.

Bolan caught Leo's wrist and turned. Again he yanked the man's arm straight, but this time he brought his forearm crashing into the outside of Leo's elbow like an iron bar. Leo's elbow didn't hyperextend this time. It shattered, and his forearm folded back the wrong way. Leo screamed as he fell, his useless arms unable to prevent him from falling into the corner of a table facefirst.

Bolan strode across the bar to the suit at the table. The man hadn't moved. He was still wearing his sunglasses. He raised his hands and smiled at Bolan in mock surrender. He spoke with a French accent. "Hey, man. No harm, no foul. You win, okay?"

Bolan closed in.

The man straightened in his chair. "Listen! I didn't do anything!"

Bolan's face was as cold as a tombstone. "You should've."

The suit dropped his hands and went for something underneath his jacket.

Bolan's fist shot across the table and crashed into the man's face. The sunglasses snapped in two and blood spurted as the septum beneath snapped as well. The back of the man's head hit the wall with bone-cracking force. He sagged forward facedown into his whiskey and then slid to a heap on the floor.

Bolan knelt beside him with his back to the crowd. He took the small, automatic pistol from the gangster's belt and slipped it into his pocket.

The bartender raised his voice wearily. "I'm calling the police."

He was a little late. Bolan nodded. "We're gone."

The policewoman glared, waving at the surrounding carnage.

Bolan jerked his head at the door. "We're gone."

Antonetti shook her head angrily but followed Bolan outside. Once they were on the street she exploded. "How about some arrests? How about assault and battery? We've got these guys cold, and you want to walk!"

"The guys on the floor are nobodies. They'll have rap sheets. Assault and battery, maybe extortion and racketeering that got plea-bargained away. They've probably done some time. But all they'll know is that they were paid to stomp a mudhole in me. They're cutouts. It's the suit at the door who's the real fish."

"Yeah, and you smashed his face in." Antonetti regarded Bolan sourly. "Unprovoked, I might add."

"He said 'Get him!' didn't he?"

"A defense attorney will chalk that up to good-natured cheerleading."

Bolan carefully pulled the little pistol he had confiscated out of his pocket.

The Mountie shook her head again. "Yeah, and you beat him up, unprovoked, and took it. It's possession, but it's inadmissible in court."

"I don't want him in court, Sergeant. I want you to run this gun for prints and ID the guy. I want to know who he is, and more than that I want to see where he goes and who he talks to. He probably won't know anything either, but his superiors might. If they don't, then the wiseguys above them."

Antonetti suddenly grinned. "We follow it right up the chain."

"You got it."

She looked Bolan up and down with new respect. "You are good."

"So are you. Tomorrow I'm going to tell your superiors that we've developed a good working rapport and that I want you to be my liaison with the RCMP." Bolan smiled. "You want the job?"

Antonetti blushed happily. "Sure."

4

"Bingo."

They were sitting in a quiet coffee shop. Information began scrolling across the screen of Sergeant Antonetti's laptop. "The pistol is an Italian Bernadelli P6. There's no record of it being imported or sold in Canada and no record of it being stolen. Its serial number indicates it was manufactured last year, so I'm betting it was smuggled into Canada directly."

Bolan had already figured out that much just by looking at it. "And the submachine guns the goons were using at the hospital were all Spectre M4s, Italian imports again, and not legally sold in North America without special permits. What about the fingerprints?"

"The lab got two clear fingerprints and a partial off the pistol. They belong to…" Antonetti punched a key, "this individual."

An RCMP rap sheet popped up on the screen.

The mug shot in the corner matched the guy directing traffic at Remy's. Bolan read the man's file. Guy Jegou, aka Guy "The Wolf" Jegou, had been arrested for racketeering and conspiracy but had beaten the rap each time. Five years ago, the Wolf had been arrested on an assault with a deadly weapon charge. It seemed a man who was in The Wolf's debt had been late with his payments too many times. Jegou had pistol-whipped him into unconsciousness and partial paralysis. His team of attorneys had plea-bargained away the assault charge, and Jegou was sentenced to a year on weapons possession, but the sentence had been suspended. Jegou was a partner in a local cement company, which was subsidiary of a construction consortium in Montreal. He had been unable to explain a substantial portion of his income, and his accountants were currently in a battle with the Canada Revenue Agency.

Bolan's assessment was that "The Wolf" stank like lower management Mafia. Loan-sharking and numbers would be his bread and butter. Bolan took in the rest of Jegou's rap sheet.

"He's not with the Italian Mob," he said.

"No." Antonetti leaned back and drank her coffee. "There are several major players in Canadian organized crime. One group is the Italians. They've been here for a century. Then in the 1990s there was a big wave of Russian immigration. The Mafia came with them. They've been aggressive and made a big impact. Canada has also had a large influx of Asians and people from the Indian subcontinent, but their criminals keep a low profile and tend to commit their crimes within their own ethnic communities.

"That leaves the French."

"Yeah, the Union Corse. They've always been here. Probably since the first French sailing ship landed. The French Mafia in Canada is an offshoot of the Union

Corse. The Corsicans have a big influence. The heroin factories in Marseilles ship directly to Quebec. They also run a lot of guns. Mostly out of Italy, as we've seen, but in recent years they've been importing a lot of surplus Serbian and Croatian weapons. Of course, the Corsicans and the Sicilians have a lot in common, and they've been known to cooperate on occasion."

Bolan nodded. In many ways, the Italian Mafia had gone soft. They still talked a good fight, and many of them were still making money, but they were on the decline. They were not the soldiers they had once been. Their code of honor had eroded, and once arrested they often turned state's evidence on one another. The Colombian, Russian, Mexican and Jamaican gangs had carved out huge chunks of their territory, particularly in the drug trade. Many of the old Families had gone completely legit. But the Union Corse and their cousins in Canada had not gone for any of that. They still killed anyone who came into their territory without an invitation or a lucrative offer of shared profit.

"Where's Jegou now?"

"Our guy watching the back followed him when he left Remy's. Thor, Leo and their buddies went to the emergency room. Our man said Jegou went home and taped his own face, but first he made a call at a pay phone. He's holed up in his house in Quidi Vidi. It's just outside St. John's."

The Wolf had undoubtedly earned his nickname. Bolan had beaten him unconscious and taken his gun.

The Wolf would want a reckoning.

Bolan was counting on it.

"Let's go see the doctor and see what he's got."

Quidi Vidi, Newfoundland

"MOTHERFUCKER." The Wolf gingerly brought a hand to his mangled face as he looked in the vanity mirror. He'd bled through the bandage across his nose again. He'd had a large nose before. Now it was squashed across his face like a crushed squid. He hawked and spit blood into the sink. "I want this Yankee piece of shit dead! You hear me?"

"Yeah, yeah, yeah. I know." Scott Clylan rolled a cigarette in one hand and checked the loads in his .357 Magnum Manurhin revolver with the other. He was a big man in a white T-shirt and a leather vest. Collections were his specialty. He'd been babysitting The Wolf for four hours, and he didn't like anything he'd heard about the situation. He snapped the revolver's cylinder shut and dug out his lighter. "They should have sent Carlo or The Moor."

"They sent the Jew," a voice said.

"Jesus!" Clylan half reached for his revolver.

"Fuck!" Jegou's nose started bleeding again as his blood pressure went through the roof "Mr. Siderisi!"

Jerome "The Jew" Siderisi stood in the doorway smiling. The Jew was a "fixer." His smile was often the last thing anyone ever saw. "So, Wolf, tell me what happened."

"Jesus!" Jegou began waving his arms. "You should have seen this fucking guy! He was the fucking Terminator. He put Thor, Leo, Fronsac and Bihan in hospital! With his bare fucking hands!" he told the rest of the story.

The Jew looked The Wolf up and down. "And he dropped you, as well? And you were heavy?"

Jegou had not told anyone his gun had been stolen from him. He sure as hell wasn't going to tell Siderisi. The Jew didn't like fuck-ups. It was one of the reasons he was such a good fixer. He had a genuine passion for erasing mistakes.

"He got the drop on me." Jegou wiped blood from his lip. "And he had some kung-fu bitch with him. She judo-chopped Bihan in the neck. Like in the movies." Jegou made a tomahawk chop motion with his hand. "Dropped him like a fucking rock."

"Is that true?" Siderisi did some math. "She was a cop. Probably RCMP. They were following our boy as well. He probably made her. He made you, too. He ducked into Remy's to sort out who his tails were." Siderisi shook his head. "Shit."

"Fuck," Clylan said in agreement.

"He's in bed with the goddamned Mounties," Siderisi calculated. "Wolf, would you recognize this bitch again?"

"Yeah, shit yeah." Jegou leered through his mangled face. "She was hot."

The Jew nodded. He had a connection that could help. He wanted this bitch's account settled. But for the moment, he had more pressing business. "Scott, how many hitters can you line up?"

"Shit, Jerome." Clylan blew smoke unhappily. "We've lost half the hitters on the Rock in the last two days, and we never had that many to begin with."

"Get as many together as you can. Anyone who isn't afraid to get wet." Siderisi raised an eyebrow. "Anyone who's ready to move up."

Clylan began punching numbers into his phone.

Jegou grinned. "We're going to whack this fuck?"

"Yeah, but not now. Right now we have other priorities."

Jegou bared his teeth. "What other fucking priorities?"

"We have other priorities. That's all you need to know, Guy." The Jew smiled.

The Wolf shut his mouth.

Clylan lowered his phone. "So what do I tell them?"

"Tell them we're going on a little road trip." Siderisi smiled with genuine amusement.

Jegou cleared his throat. "Scotty, get me a gun."

Clylan stubbed out his cigarette. "You have a gun."

Siderisi's eyes narrowed.

Jegou pointed at his face. "I want a bigger one."

The Jew shook his head in amused disgust. "Scotty, get him a bigger fucking gun."

"Right." Clylan waved his phone. "So where do I tell the boys we're going?"

"Tell them we're gonna go to Trinity Bay." Siderisi's smile turned dangerous again. "Tell them we're gonna meet Carlo."

"Jesus." Jegou swallowed with difficulty. He definitely wanted a bigger gun.

"WHAT HAVE YOU GOT?"

Bolan and Antonetti sat in Dr. Ferentinos's office. Aaron Kurtzman joined them via a laptop and a satellite link. "The Bear" had been doing his own research into the problem back in Virginia.

Dr. Ferentinos glanced at the RCMP report and then at Bolan and Antonetti. "The dental records came back. Forensics had a positive ID on one of our victims. His name was Sylvan Prettys. He's one of the ones who died during the attack."

Bolan glanced at the man's picture. "You have a residence on him?"

"Yes, Cape Breton, Nova Scotia."

Antonetti scanned the police file that came with the report. "Prettys is suspected of being connected to organized crime in Nova Scotia. Real lower tier stuff. He was arrested for suspected truck hijacking. He beat that and a year later was convicted on grand theft auto. He did two years."

"What's he been up to lately?"

"Not much." She flipped through the file. "He did his time. He was on parole and stayed clean. When he got out of jail, he got himself a job, an apartment and a dog. According to his parole officer, he's been an exemplary parolee. His employer says the same. No violations until a week and a half ago when he didn't show up for his regularly scheduled meeting." Antonetti closed the file. "He's been missing ever since."

"Missing since he got infected." Bolan corrected. "The question is, how did he come into contact with the bacteria and where?"

Dr. Ferentinos leaned back in his chair. "It sounds like you're assuming he didn't come into contact with the disease here in Newfoundland, but all known cases have occurred right here on the Rock. If the victims were exposed to the bacteria somewhere else, why are there no reports of outbreaks from any other provinces or territories?"

"Your problem is you're thinking this through like an epidemiologist." Bolan said. "You're following the bacteria."

Ferentinos stared at Bolan. "Well, you got me there. What are you following?"

"I'm following human behavior. What we've seen leads me to think that everyone else infected with the bacteria or connected with the outbreak is dead, and I mean murdered, to keep it quiet."

"I suppose that is a possibility, given the circumstances," the doctor admitted.

"Our first victim, Sylvan, and his unknown associate were running. When they got so sick they were brought into the hospital, the people looking for them found out about it and came for them. They came with guns, as you'll recall."

"Right." Ferentinos was still coming to grips with the fact that he had been in a gunfight in his own hospital. "So, we're out of leads then?"

"Not at all. We know the Canadian Mafia, in particular the French-Canadian Mafia, is somehow involved. We need to find out who at the top is pulling the strings here on the Rock." Bolan turned to the video screen and Kurtzman. The cybernetic team leader had been crunching data at Stony Man Farm in Virginia. "How many Mafia Families do we have in Canada, Bear?"

"Dozens and dozens. The majority are clustered in the provincial and territorial capitals, the big cities, and cities along the U.S. border."

"Find any that have any kind of link with pharmaceutical labs, starting in Canada, and limit the search to no farther south than Mexico."

Kurtzman sighed. "That's going to be a needle in a haystack."

"Find it, Bear. Find me anything. I don't care how tenuous it is. Right now, all we have is The Wolf, and he isn't high up enough to be of any use unless he can lead us to somebody bigger."

"I'm on it. I've got the whole team on it."

Ferentinos rubbed his wounded shoulder. "Listen, they came with guns, I know. That goes a long way toward your theory that the bacteria has been weaponized, but I've got to tell you, we're still not rock solid on that. It appears that the bacteria is dependent on a significant contact vector. Like these guys got it spilled on them directly or something. I think we all agree that the effects are hideous, and as a terror device, well, they've shut down an entire Canadian province."

"That was an accident." Bolan nodded. "But?"

"But still, if it has been weaponized, well, it's a lousy weapon."

"For now."

"For now?"

"I suspected they've mutated the bacteria, and they're not finished. I think they had an accident with it while it was still in the oven. I want you to imagine it when they stick a fork in it and it's done. When you can catch it off a doorknob, by rubbing your eyes, getting coughed on, or having it genuinely airborne."

Worst-case scenarios began playing like horror movies in Dr. Ferentinos's head. "Right," he said.

"Doctor. I'm here to deal with the people who started this, but you're the lead man on the bacteria itself," Bolan said.

Ferentinos nodded.

"You're a target." Bolan reached down to his ankle holster. Velcro sounded as he drew a snub-nosed 9 mm Smith & Wesson Centennial revolver and set it on the doctor's desk. "Five shots, loaded and ready to go, just point it and pull the trigger."

"Umm, that's not…" Antonetti sighed and looked away. "I didn't see that."

Ferentinos looked at the revolver on his desk like it was a snake.

Bolan nodded slowly. "I know you have issues with it, Doctor. You're sworn to save lives. But I have issues with the flesh rotting off the bones of an entire province. You have two jobs. One is to beat the bacteria, the other is to stay alive long enough to do it."

Ferentinos took a deep breath and let it out slowly.

"Besides—" Bolan lightened his tone. "—I saw you with the assault rifle. You're a natural."

Ferentinos snorted. "Can I have one of those, instead?"

"You'll have to ask her."

Antonetti shook her head. "You know, I'm just going to close my eyes and pretend this conversation never happened," she replied.

Ferentinos slid the little revolver into his pocket. "Thanks."

"Okay." Antonetti raised her eyebrows. "If you're done passing out party favors, what's your next grand idea?"

"We need to push it. The Wolf is our only solid lead at the moment. We need him to run to the big fish or bring them in." Bolan rose from his chair. "I say we go and goose him along."

5

Quidi Vidi, Newfoundland

"You can't just kick the door down and beat the answers out of them." Sergeant Antonetti stood with Bolan on the porch outside Jegou's home. It was early morning, and the breeze was blowing cold off of the black water of the harbor. "We at least need probable cause."

"You're right. We'll have to be subtle about this." Bolan drew his pistol with a shrug and knocked on the door.

A voice snarled from within. "Who is it?"

"The guy who stepped on your face, Wolf," the Executioner said.

Antonetti drew her P 226 service pistol and prudently stepped to one side.

"Fuck you!" The Wolf screamed. "Die!"

His pistol sounded like dynamite detonating.

Splinters flew. Bolan eyed the three ragged holes in the door at chest height. They were big enough to put your thumb through. "He got himself a bigger gun," Bolan said. He regarded Antonetti as two more bullets punched through the door. The report of the weapon rattled the windowpanes. "You got probable cause yet?"

"Yeah." Antonetti grimaced as voices shouted at each other from within. More guns began firing through the door. "And he's got friends."

"So do I." Bolan reached into his pocket and pulled out a black and red cylinder as big as a tall-size beer can and pulled the pin. He opened his hand, and the cotter pin pinged away. "Cover your ears and look away."

Antonetti covered her ears.

Bolan walked down the little porch. He rammed his gloved fist through the front window and opened his hand. He spun away as gunfire answered back.

The men inside shouted in sudden panic.

The stun grenade detonated and the remaining windows blew out from the pressure. Much worse for occupants of the room was the sudden candlepower flash, 185 decibels of sound and the secondary pyrotechnic display.

Bolan kicked in the front door. Thousands of sparks were drifting about the room like drunken fireflies. Three armed men stood in the room reeling like drunks themselves, blinded, deafened and disoriented. One of the men held another of the smuggled submachine guns. The weapon blazed into life, burning its 50-round magazine in a wide arc as its half-blind wielder swept for targets. Bolan put a burst into his chest. The man turned pale and sat down gasping.

Antonetti's pistol barked behind Bolan, and the second man staggered backward as he took three rounds in the torso and fell to the floor.

Guy Jegou staggered around waving a stainless-steel snub-nosed .44 Magnum pistol. The gun clicked repeatedly as he kept pulling the trigger on empty chambers.

The Wolf was too disoriented to realize he'd shot his gun dry. Bolan strode forward and drove the butt of his Beretta into Jegou's face.

Jegou screamed as the pistol crashed into his wounded face. He dropped his weapon and fell to his knees clutching his head. Antonetti checked the other rooms. The home was clear.

The Wolf screamed as Bolan seized him by the hair and heaved him to his feet. "You're dead! You hear me? You fucking American piece of—"

Bolan chicken-winged Jegou's arm and marched him into the bathroom.

Jegou screamed again as Bolan hurled him through the glass door of the shower stall.

Antonetti had called the paramedics and was administering first aid to the wheezing gangster with the holes in his chest. "Torturing suspects isn't—"

"This man has been subjected to a stun munition. I'm treating him for possible burns." Bolan yanked out the tap and turned it all the way over to Cold.

Jegou jerked and spasmed as the icy water blasted him. The water turned a frigid, frothy pink as he bled from his numerous lacerations. "Okay! Shit! Fuck! Ok—"

The cold water sizzled and hissed off the barrel of Bolan's machine pistol. He pressed the muzzle between Jegou's raccooning eyes.

"Okay," the guy whimpered.

"The water's cold, Wolf, but the Atlantic is a lot colder. And if you think you're ugly now, the oldest fisherman in Newfoundland is going to throw up when he sees what the crabs have done to your face when you come up in the nets." The machine pistol clicked with cold finality as the lever was flicked to single shot. "Give me a name!" Bolan thundered.

"The Jew!" Jegou screamed. "You want The Jew!"

"Where?"

"Trinity Bay! He's going to fucking Trinity Bay!" Jegou shuddered at the enormity of his betrayal.

Bolan said, "Tell me everything."

"I don't know anything!" Jegou shrieked.

Sirens wailed in the distance.

Guy "The Wolf" Jegou began babbling like a brook.

Trinity Bay

BOLAN SAW IT, but he almost couldn't believe it. He stopped the car and folded his arms across his chest as he looked at the sign. "Dildo?"

"Yup." Antonetti nodded.

"The town's name really is Dildo?"

Through the trees Bolan could hear a live band playing. He checked the loads in his machine pistol.

They'd gleaned some information from Jegou but not enough. Jerome "The Jew" Siderisi had a long history in Canadian organized crime. He was suspected in a number of gangland-style slayings. Like most of his ilk, he had never been convicted of anything major. The Wolf had been waiting for someone to come pick him up. Who they were he wasn't sure, and since The Wolf's baby-sitters hadn't checked in, Bolan suspected that whoever they were they would not be arriving in Quidi Vidi any time soon. The Jew had gone to Trinity Bay to meet someone. The only name Jegou had was "Carlo," and he'd whispered it with reverential awe.

Bolan girded his mental loins and drove into Dildo.

The town was gorgeous. It looked like a lot of other fishing towns on the East Coast. Clapboard houses were nestled in the low, rolling hills around the harbor. Picture postcard conifers stood here and there, gradually thickening into stands of pine forest.

Banners were strung everywhere proclaiming civic pride. There were a startling number of people from out of town. They were easy to spot. Nearly all of them sported T-shirts with the name of the town boldly emblazoned on them and couldn't stop posing beside every sign with the town name and taking pictures. Some sort of street festival aimed at tourists was underway.

They got out of the car and began walking. A lot of the action seemed to be taking place in and around the outdoor public pool. Children ran everywhere. Music was playing, and vendors were serving food and selling souvenirs and local handicrafts. There were pony rides and face painting, and a clown was handing out balloons. People were clustered around the stage dancing to the live music, and the beer tent was seeing heavy traffic. It was Saturday afternoon, and the celebration was kicking into high gear. The state of emergency on the Rock didn't seem to be affecting the fun in Dildo.

Antonetti looked like she wanted to join the festivities. "Let's look around a bit," Bolan said.

Bolan stopped at a table and picked up a free pamphlet describing the wonders of Dildo. The town's distinctive name was thought to be Portuguese. For most of its history, fishing, whaling and later mink farming had been the lifeblood of the town.

Bolan was pleased as he scanned the pamphlet. Three founding families had settled the town of Dildo in the early 1800s. Those families were the Reids, the Smiths and the Prettys. They were still the predominant names in the community today.

"Dani."

Antonetti scanned the pamphlet. "You're right, the victims were running. When people run, they run for home and they run for family."

"Almost always."

"They couldn't have gotten here directly from Cape Breton. They would have had to fly or take a ferry into St. John's. By that time they were too ill to continue."

"That's the way I see it," Bolan agreed. "Almost all Mafias are family operations. Even at the lowest levels. If Siderisi and this mystery killer Carlo are here, they're here to whack somebody, and I'm betting they're relatives of Sylvan's."

Antonetti handed the pamphlet back. "Well, we've got three founding families, about eighteen hundred citizens, and that leaves about, oh, six hundred possible relatives to sift through."

"Yeah."

Bolan spied a police constable on a mountain bike handing out police trading cards to a cluster of children with painted faces. "Why don't you go talk to the constable over there while I try the chamber."

"Good idea," Antonetti said and headed off.

Bolan went over to the Dildo Chamber of Commerce

table. A man sat behind it with a name badge that read "Lou Reid, Executive Director, Dildo Chamber of Commerce." He sat gazing benevolently at the proceedings.

Bolan smiled and waved his hand in an all-encompassing gesture of the festival. "Quite a civic celebration you have here."

"Thanks!" Lou appeared to have more than a few drinks in him. "You're an American?" he asked.

Bolan sighed. "Am I that easy to spot?"

Lou waved his beer magnanimously. "It doesn't make you a bad person."

"Thanks."

"So what brings you to our town?" Lou winked. "Don't tell me we're already famous in the States."

"Not yet, actually I'm here on family business." Bolan gestured back at Antonetti. She and her fellow Mountie were leaning close as they talked. "My wife's Canadian, from St. John's. We're looking for a cousin of hers."

"Well, it's a small town." Lou admired Antonetti's behind.

"You know Sylvan Prettys?" Bolan asked.

Lou's face fell. "You know, you're the second person who's asked me that today."

"Really? Who else?"

"His parole officer." Lou looked Bolan up and down suspiciously. "Why are you looking for him?"

Bolan shrugged and began ad-libbing. "Well, actually, that's something I wanted to speak to you about as well. I'm from Pennsylvania, and I own two microbreweries there. My wife has always wanted one of her own, and she wants to start her business up here in Canada." Bolan grinned. "She thinks Dildo Pale Ale has a ring to it. We were just in Quidi Vidi, and their microbrewery is doing very well. I think she might have a good idea."

"Really?" Lou suddenly became very animated. "Dildo Microbrew! That's a hell of an idea!"

"We think so. Anyway, we knew her cousin Sylvan had been in some trouble. We thought we might put him in on the ground floor. You know, give him a new start."

"Well, now, that's decent of you," Lou Reed conceded. "Sylvan and his cousins, they got into some trouble around here as kids. They grew up and went to St. John's and got in more trouble. Rumor has it they went to Cape Breton and got themselves into real trouble. I heard Sylvan did time."

Bolan sighed sadly. "Two years."

"Well, last I heard he had a job at a distillery. Haven't heard much of him since."

Distillery. Bolan filed that away. "What about the cousins?"

"The twins?" Lou shrugged. "I haven't seen or heard of Baron and Ames in ten years. I'd hoped not to. Black sheep of the town."

Bolan needed to compare some notes. "Listen, my wife wants to dance. Give me your card. We'll talk about the project when things are a little quieter."

"Love to!" Lou eagerly slid Bolan his card.

Antonetti looked back and waved Bolan over.

"This is Constable Kubak," she said as Bolan approached.

Kubak was about 275 pounds. His shaved head gleamed in the sun. He shook Bolan's hand. His Newfoundland brogue was thick enough to cut with a knife. "Pleased to meet you, eh."

"Kubak was just telling me a bit about Sylvan. He wasn't a nice boy."

Bolan didn't need confirmation on Sylvan. He was more interested in the twins. "What about Baron and Ames?" he asked.

"The twins?" Kubak scowled. "Dirty as a duck's puddle. I beat the tar out of them twice, and that was personal, before I became a cop. Hell, shits like them made me become a cop. Ugly as sin, they were."

"If they were here, and hiding out, where do you think they might be?"

"Jeez. If they were in town, I'd know about it." Kubak rubbed his skull. "Well, their family used to have a mink farm a few kilometers inland."

"What happened to it?"

"Well, Dildo was huge into whaling until it was banned. Problem is, minks eat meat, and the mink farms here depended on the whale carcasses for tons of cheap feed. When the whaling ended, so did most of the mink farms." Kubak shrugged. "What do you feed a thousand minks? Steak? Most of the minkers went bust. I know the Prettys did. The family still owns the land, though. There are some old cabins and sheds out there."

Bolan and Antonetti exchanged looks.

Kubak waved out toward the hills. "I can take you round if you like."

"Lead on," Bolan replied.

6

Kubak pulled onto a narrow lane in the forest. A pair of trees flanked the entrance. Nailed between them above the road was an arching sign that was so weathered it was unreadable. A faded No Trespassing sign hung by a single nail. Barbed wire was strung along the tree line. As they drove in, they found a low maze of rusted chicken-wire enclosures and a number of falling-down sheds. Past the sheds sat a little A-frame cabin.

Bolan leaned forward and tapped Kubak's shoulder. "Stop."

Kubak put his cruiser in park. Bolan took out his binoculars and examined the cabin.

Antonetti frowned. "What do you see?"

"Someone's been here." Bolan scanned the front of dwelling. "There's fresh cigarette butts on the porch and beer bottles. The labels aren't discolored or peeled."

Kubak nodded. "Kids don't have to come out here to get drunk or get laid. There's a million places closer town."

"So they're here. Or they've been here." Antonetti opened her door. "How should we—"

"Down!" Bolan roared. He grabbed her collar and yanked her back into her seat. A high-powered rifle cracked, and Antonetti's window shattered inches from her face.

Kubak threw open his door and crouched behind it for cover. "That would be Baron. Ames was always gutless around guns," he said. He grabbed his transmitter and his voice thundered out from the loudspeaker on the roof of the cruiser. "Bide where you're at, Baron!"

"Fuck you!" a voice screamed from the cabin.

Bolan nodded to himself. Baron was absolutely terrified, and he was scared of a lot more than being arrested.

"Baron!" Kubak's voice boomed. "I am fair wore out with your bullshit! This can go smooth as oil or hard as the hob of hell! You choose!"

"Fuck you, Doug! Ya fat fuck!" The rifle cracked again, and bits of Kubak's shattered light bar tinkled to the gravel. "I'll kill ya!"

Constable Douglas Kubak glowered from beneath his massive brow. He did, indeed, appear to be wore out with Baron Prettys's bullshit. He pulled his shotgun off the rack and took a very deep breath. "Baron! We are the RCMP! And you've just fired twice upon us!"

Baron Prettys's voice cracked. "Oh…shit."

Antonetti shook her head. "If he was any dumber, he'd have to be bigger."

Kubak nodded at the wisdom of the statement and then roared at Baron. "Oh shit is right, Baron! Now give it up!"

Bolan weighed the panic in Baron's voice. "Constable, let me use the horn a minute."

Kubak handed over the mike.

Bolan modulated his voice to quiet concern. "Mr. Prettys, my name is Cooper. I'm the American representative with the epidemiology team at St. Clare's Hospital in St. John's. Where's your brother Ames?"

There was a long pause. "He took sick! Real sick!"

"Baron, I can have a medivac helicopter here in twenty minutes."

"They'll kill us!"

"Baron, I can have your brother in a maximum security quarantine unit, surrounded by a dozen Mounties. Assuming you're not infected, I can have you on a plane to the United States within the hour. I can have you in a five-star hotel in California with a hot tub and satellite television. I can get you in the Witness Protection program, full ride any place on Earth you want to go, but you have to play ball, and you have to do the right thing. You have to save your brother!" Bolan shrugged out of his gun leather in the back seat. He was carrying a .50-caliber Desert Eagle semiautomatic pistol with armor-piercing ammunition, and his Beretta machine pistol was chambered for 9 mm hollowpoints rather than .22s.

Bolan slid out of the car unarmed.

He held his coat open and did a slow turn. "I don't have a gun. I'm not a policeman." He held up his hands. "Let me look at your brother!"

The long barrel of a hunting rifle slid out from the cabin's shattered porch window. Bolan could see the reflection off the telescopic sight as it pointed at him.

"Okay… Okay! But the cops stay back!"

"Fine! Let me come up. Let me look at your brother. I have the authority to cut you a deal. We'll talk. You don't like the deal, I'll be your hostage."

"You fuck me, I'll kill you!"

"Let me come up onto the porch. You can stay inside."

"Fine! You come ahead, fucker! But don't try anything!"

Bolan took the long walk to the porch. Baron was crouched behind the windowsill with little more than the top of his blond head and his rifle showing. Bolan walked up the steps and deliberately put himself between Baron and the Canadian police officers.

Baron was sweating.

Bolan smiled. "Can I put my hands down?"

"Fuck you!"

It was what Bolan had figured he'd say.

Baron rose, and the Executioner stared down the barrel of a Winchester 30-06.

Baron shook like a leaf. "You're telling me you can save my brother?"

"No." Bolan slowly shook his head. "I'm not going to lie to you, Baron. I'm just investigating the situation. But I can get Ames into the best hospital in Newfoundland, and have the top bacteriologists and surgeons in North America do everything in their power to save him. Both Canada and the United States have experts pouring onto the Rock with batteries of experimental drugs. I can put your brother in the best possible care on the planet, and I can get you out of whatever situation you're in. That I can guarantee, and I give you my word, no matter what happens, I'll help your brother any way I can."

"Fuck you! You smooth talking faggot." The muzzle of the hunting rifle slid out the shattered window inches from Bolan's eyes. "I should just—"

Bolan's hand blurred.

The rifle cracked, but Bolan had already slapped the muzzle out of line. His hand closed around the hot barrel as he yanked it, half ripping the rifle from Baron's hands. The man held on to the weapon for dear life, yanking back.

Bolan didn't play tug-of-war. He let Baron have his rifle. The soldier kept his grip on the barrel and shoved with all of his might.

Baron took the butt of his own rifle between the eyes. Bolan pulled the rifle again and rammed it forward, beating it into his adversary's face a second and a third time. Baron's eyes crossed. His hands slid from the rifle's stock, and he toppled to the floor inside the cabin.

Bolan spun the rifle around like a baton. He worked the bolt and chambered a fresh round as he walked across the porch and kicked the door in.

Kubak and Antonetti came running.

"Hold it!" Bolan's nose wrinkled as he took in the interior of the cabin. The cabin stank of stale beer and cigarette smoke. But overpowering all was the stench of the rotting dead. "We may have a hot zone!" Bolan called out in warning.

Antonetti approached the porch. "I'm supposed to render you all reasonable aid and assistance, but this is a national emergency. The RCMP isn't waiting outside while a foreigner, even an ally, examines a local crime scene."

Kubak stood like a human wall with his shotgun at port arms. "Yeah."

"All right." Bolan stood away from the door. "After you."

Kubak's face tightened as they entered. "Jesus!"

Beer bottles and candy wrappers littered the filthy carpet. Flies buzzed in violent circles around the heaps of trash. Bolan went to the bedroom and checked the closet. Through the bedroom window he saw a beat up El Camino parked behind the cabin. "Clear!"

Kubak swept the bathroom and the study. "Clear!"

Antonetti rolled Baron onto his stomach and handcuffed him. "Baron, where's your brother?"

Baron Prettys's eyes struggled to focus. "Cellar...I put Ames down in the cellar."

Bolan glanced at the cellar door. The stench emanating from it was palpable. "You want me to do it?"

"No." Antonetti went to the door flanked by Kubak. Bolan frowned. Baron had bolted the door from the outside. Sergeant Antonetti shot the bolt and opened the door. "Oh...God..."

The smell hit them in a solid wave. Bolan had faced disinterred mass graves in equatorial jungles that had smelled better. Antonetti's hand grabbed the pull chain and she flicked on the light.

A single bare bulb illuminated the scene in the cellar.

Antonetti's hands shot to her mouth. She spun and staggered back into the living room. She fell to her hands and knees, vomiting. Kubak took one look at the atrocity below and bolted. He just made it to the bathroom sink as he got sick. Bolan stared down into the cellar. He couldn't blame the Canadians. He was controlling his own gorge by sheer force of will. Bolan steeled himself and examined the scene. It was fairly obvious by the litter surrounding the landing that Baron had been throwing candy and soda down to his brother Ames from the top of the stairs. Half of the food was unopened. There were several packs of cigarettes and couple of books of matches that had not been touched.

Ames Prettys lay on a filthy mattress by the bottom step. His decomposition was so horrific it was hard to tell where Ames left off and his crumpled and stained bedding began. Bolan's face was stone as he stared at the putrefying corpse at the bottom of the stairs.

"Hey! You gotta help my brother!" Baron Prettys tried to sit up.

Kubak came out of the bathroom, green around the gills but with his revolver in his hand. Antonetti stared at Bolan in shock.

Bolan crossed the room in three strides. He put his foot into Baron's chest and pinned him against the wall.

Baron's eyes bugged. "You—"

The man gagged on steel as Bolan shoved the barrel of the rifle into his mouth. Bolan's eyes blazed as his voice went Arctic. "I think you know what your brother was sick with, and I think you know where he got it. I think you knew you should've taken him to a hospital the second he got sick, and then there might have been a chance to save him. Instead you threw your brother down into a cellar and left him down there to die in the dark. Half the food down there hasn't been touched. How many days has it been since Ames couldn't feed himself?"

Bolan leaned on the rifle hard. Baron gagged.

"Your brother was dying in agony, and you threw starvation and dehydration into the mix." Baron shrieked around steel as Bolan threw the bolt and chambered a fresh round. "You don't deserve any mercy."

Bolan took his foot off Baron's clavicles and yanked the rifle out of his mouth. Baron collapsed to the floor, shuddering and weeping. Bolan kicked the door open and stepped out onto the porch to get some air.

Kubak followed Bolan out a few moments later. He stared long and hard at the Executioner. "Dude, you are hard core." The big Mountie shook his head. "And I hope I never see the place that made you that way."

Bolan nodded. Constable Kubak was a perceptive man. Bolan could tell he was a good cop.

Antonetti came out onto the porch and leaned against the railing to steady herself.

Bolan looked at the others. "Baron is alive, and at the moment he's enough of an emotional mess to spill his guts. He's our one lead on where this all started, and there's at least half a platoon of Union Corse hitters in the area looking to shut him up. We need to get him out of here now."

Kubak holstered his pistol. "Shouldn't we quarantine him? I mean, maybe we should quarantine all of us."

"If Baron had the bacteria in his system, he'd be showing symptoms by now. I'm betting he's all right. I'm guessing however his brother got exposed didn't happen to him. We need to get him into protective custody and in the hands of RCMP interrogators immediately."

"Right." Antonetti stood tall and wiped her chin with her fist. "Right."

Bolan turned to Kubak. "Constable, from what I saw there's basically two roads in and out of town. You need to get on the horn and set up checkpoints on either side. Two of the hitters have been identified as Jerome Siderisi and Scott Clylan. The sergeant can get you photos and descriptions. Tell your men that these people are Mafia hit men, armed and dangerous and looking to clip somebody. Have your officers heavily armed. Meanwhile, let's get police tape around the house and at the entrance to the farm."

"You got it."

Bolan went back inside the cabin. Baron Prettys sobbed hysterically on the floor. He yipped as Bolan yanked him to his feet. "Let's go." He walked Baron bawling and stumbling back to the cruiser. The two Canadian officers finished taping the crime scene, and they drove back toward town. Both of them got busy on the car radio. Antonetti leaned back in her seat. "Helicopters are on the way, ETA fifteen minutes. One of them is carrying Dr. Ferentinos and his team. The doctor says he tentatively agrees with your threat assessment, but we have to be sure. He doesn't want any of us leaving the area until he can run blood tests. He says that with field equipment he should be able to determine if Baron or any of us have the bacteria in our bloodstream within an hour."

Bolan nodded as they approached the Dildo Corral.

Kubak checked his watch. "The local detachments are sending two dozen constables to reinforce the roadblocks, and they should start pouring into town in about ten minutes."

"We have fifty RCMP officers on the way from the capital," Antonetti added. "They should be here within the hour."

Bolan cleared leather. "Look out!" he shouted.

Kubak jerked the steering wheel, but there was no time. "Jesus! Hold on—"

The Ford Bronco broke out of the bushes and rammed the cruiser broadside. The car lurched across the one lane road and sideswiped a tree. Kubak's brow bled from where it had bounced on the door frame, but he grimly held on and fought the wheel. Baron Prettys screamed as bullets began striking the car. The cruiser fishtailed as the Bronco clipped their rear bumper. The cruiser started to slide sideways. There was a turn up ahead. In a moment, they would be pinned between the Bronco and an oncoming tree.

Kubak stomped on the accelerator, and the Chevy shot into the corral. One of the door panels buckled as they struck a tree trunk framing the entrance. The cruiser lurched and went diagonal on the access road. The front bumper clipped a tree, and the car spun out of control. The front tires went out over empty space and then crashed down into the drainage ditch. The engine made a sound like a dying beast as the drive train snapped.

"Out." Bolan lunged out of the teetering car. "Everyone out!"

The Bronco overshot the corral. At the entrance, it came reversing into view. It oriented itself onto the corral road and lurched forward spitting gravel, its V-8 engine roaring like a juggernaut.

"Get him out of here!" Bolan pulled a flash-stun grenade from his jacket. He vainly wished he had a frag or an antiarmor grenade as he pulled the pin. The munition would have no effect on a truck.

But the driver didn't know that.

Bolan flung the grenade at the oncoming Bronco.

The driver braked, and the grenade detonated three feet from the grille. Blinding light flashed and the stun weapon made a noise like a naval deck gun going off. The Bronco swerved wildly through the disorienting sparks. It smashed into a line of saplings by the road, and the nose suddenly dropped as the front wheels fell into the ditch. The Bronco's back tires lifted momentarily, then fell back to the ground. Steam came from under the hood and the idling engine hissed and ticked. The big four by four had survived the axle-snapping drop.

Bolan drew his Desert Eagle pistol. The huge pistol thundered in his hands as he methodically emptied the seven round magazine of armor-piercing ammo into the body of the Bronco.

Bolan reloaded and raced down the road for the corral.

"SON OF A BITCH!"

The Jew flung himself out of the Bronco and dropped to the ground. Two of his men were dead. A third was in the backseat screaming with his left arm hanging from his shoulder by bloody strings. Siderisi unlocked the folding stock of his SPAS-12 shotgun. He was a fixer. He scanned the road ahead from beneath the Ford. The cruiser had been abandoned.

"Shit!" Scott Clylan dropped down beside him. "He's got fucking bombs!"

"No, Scotty." Siderisi shook his head. "That was a fucking cracker. Stun grenade. Cops and special forces faggots use them in hostage situations. I've seen that shit on The Learning Channel."

"Stun grenades?" Clylan shoved a fresh clip into his Uzi. "We don't got stun grenades, Jerome."

"We have lead, Scotty." Siderisi was smiling again. "And we've got Carlo." The Jew flicked open his phone and punched in a number. It was answered on the first ring. A voice spoke with a thick French accent.

"I heard the gunfire. Where are you?"

Siderisi shook his head in disgust. "The Dildo fucking Corral."

"It is done, no?"

"No, the fucking American you warned us about showed up. He has that Mountie bitch with him and the biggest fucking RCMP constable you ever saw." Siderisi glanced behind him. "You heard the shooting? Where are you?"

"I'm at the Prettys's mink farm. There's police tape at the entrance and around the cabin. I must have missed them by about a minute."

"They have one of the twins with them. I think it's Baron. You see any sign of Ames?"

"Ames is in basement. He's applesauce."

"SHIT!" ANTONETTI GLANCED around the stable helplessly. "The horses are gone."

"They'll be down at the festival." Kubak peered out the back door. "There's no cars here, either."

Behind the stable was about fifty yards of thinning trees, and then the land opened up into low rolling hills that stopped at the sea. The four-wheel-drive Bronco could chase them down with ease.

Antonetti was peering between the slats of the stable wall. "They're coming."

"Shit!" Baron was close to hysterics again. "They're gonna kill us! They're gonna fuckin' kill us all and—" Baron shut up as Bolan's gaze fell upon him.

Bolan looked through the crack. The hitters were coming. They'd gotten their Bronco out of the ditch, but it was hanging back by the entrance. The killers were moving forward at a crouch down the drainage ditches on either side of the corral road. All of them were carrying a shotgun or submachine gun. Bolan wished he'd kept Baron's hunting rifle. "I count seven, plus at least one behind the wheel of the Bronco.

"So what do we do?" Antonetti asked.

"In about fifteen seconds, they're going to start spreading out and putting the stable in a crossfire. I'm going to step out before that happens. You two go out the back and come around either side of the stable."

"You're just going to walk out there and start shooting?" Kubak was incredulous.

"Yeah." Bolan pulled a grenade from his jacket. He had been expecting to be the besieger rather than the besieged, but it was the only surprise card he had left to play. "Go out the back and count to ten. The wind is off the water, but be careful. This is CS tear gas, not CN. It's military strength." He jerked his head at the back door. "Go."

The Canadian officers moved.

Baron Prettys sat in the hay wide-eyed with terror.

"You. Stay out of sight." Bolan pulled the pin on his grenade and kicked open the stable door. Muzzles swung in his direction. Bolan flung the grenade. It hit the ground and broke into multiple skip-chasing bomblets. The three submunitions bounced and skipped in opposite directions on their spewing jets of irritant gas.

A shotgun roared off to Bolan's left, and he felt the wind of the buckshot pattern's passage. The Beretta 93-R snarled off a 3-round burst that printed a triangle pattern of craters in the shooter's skull.

A curtain of gray gas covered the entrance of the corral. Guns began going off from all directions. Bolan raised both pistols and began shooting in earnest. These men were Mafia hitters, and he was depending on that fact. The vast majority of gangsters were assassins, not soldiers. Murder was their MO. They came to their targets smiling or from behind in dark alleys. A standing gunfight was their last, worst option.

Battle experience and body armor were Bolan's main advantage.

The Executioner stood and shot.

A blast of buckshot took him square in the chest. The Executioner staggered. A second blast knocked him to one knee. He squeezed the machine pistol's trigger three times, and nine rounds of 9 mm ammo walked up the killer's torso from his crotch to his collar.

The Bronco came roaring down the road.

Kubak and Antonetti were firing from either side of the stable.

Bolan stood as the Bronco blasted through the gas cloud and bore down on him like a battering ram. The Executioner leveled the Desert Eagle and printed three rounds at head level through the driver's-side windshield. The windshield spiderwebbed with cracks and went opaque. With Bolan's fourth round the glass suddenly smeared in a spray of red.

Bolan stepped aside as the Bronco plowed out of control through the stable wall.

Baron began screaming hysterically.

A third shotgun blast smashed Bolan in the side. His lungs cringed in his chest, and he felt the burn and tug of a bullet strike in his left bicep. The Beretta fell from his hand as he wobbled to one knee again. Bolan put his front sight on the shotgunner and fired. The Desert Eagle boomed and clacked open on a smoking empty chamber.

The man toppled back into the drainage ditch.

Kubak's voice roared. "Are you all—"

A pair of pistols boomed. Kubak fell against a fence post.

A rifle fired from somewhere outside of the firefight.

"Sniper!" Antonetti screamed. "Sniper!"

A big man in a leather vest came out of the gas cloud. Tears streamed down his swollen face. He carried a smoking .357 Magnum revolver in each hand. He staggered toward Bolan hacking and coughing.

Bolan pulled his bootknife free of its ankle sheath with a rasp. He whipped his arm around like a softball fast pitch, and the four inches of anodized skeleton steel flew.

The revolvers roared. Bolan's heart made a fist as he took the bullets dead center. The man's reddened eyes flew wide as the knife punched up under his jaw. His jaw worked soundlessly as his glottis stopped on steel.

The man dropped to his knees. He blinked at Bolan in incomprehension and fell on his face.

Bolan rolled behind a water trough as a rifle bullet kicked up dust by his knee. He struggled to draw a fresh magazine and reload the Desert Eagle one-handed. It was hard work to draw breath past the bruising he had taken under his armor.

"Shit! Fuck! Shit!" Baron Prettys ran out of the half-collapsed stable like a chicken with its head cut off, screaming and handcuffed. "Fuck! Fuck! Fuck!"

Bolan would have shouted if he could draw breath. He would have winged Baron if he'd had a loaded gun.

"Down, asshole!" Antonetti screamed. It didn't occur to the RCMP sergeant to wing him.

The rifle in the woods cracked. Baron staggered and slowed as if an invisible fist had punched him between the shoulder blades. The rifle fired a second time, and Baron's head blew apart like a water balloon. His knees went limp, and he toppled into the dust.

Bolan shoved the slide release, and his pistol clacked closed on a fresh round. "Kubak!"

Kubak leaned against the side of the stable. He was out of sight of the sniper, but he didn't look good. His face was white, and his right arm was bleeding a river. "I'm all right! I think…"

"Sit tight!" Bolan craned his head around to try to find Antonetti, but she was behind cover. "Dani! The sniper! Where's the sniper?"

"He's in the trees! I can't see him! But I saw the flash of his second shot! He's about a hundred meters in and—"

The rifleman suddenly began firing in a rapid string. Bolan noted that he had to have a semiautomatic rifle.

"Son of a bitch!" Kubak was shocked. The sniper was shooting the wounded men laying about the stableyard.

Bolan tore a strip from the hem of his shirt and used his teeth to help bind his left bicep.

One hundred meters was not ideal but it was close enough, he thought. "Dani! Get back in the stable. See if that truck can still run! If it does, you and Kubak head for the hills. If the sniper shoots, I'll try and take him!"

"Right!"

Kubak moved around the stable toward the back. Antonetti yelled from inside. "Move!"

Her service gun started firing in a rapid string.

Bolan rolled to his feet.

The water trough geysered water from a bullet strike but Bolan was already up and running. He dived for the side of the stable. Splinters flew as a bullet sought his head.

Bolan rolled flat to the ground and waited until he heard an engine revving.

Timbers flew as the Bronco burst through the frame of the door. Bolan ran around the back of the sagging stable. The vehicle was lurching and steaming, but it was heading into the hills.

A blond man with a rifle emerged at the edge of the tree line. It was the man from the hospital. The assassin began emptying his weapon at the fleeing truck as fast as he could pull the trigger. Bolan dropped to one knee. The range was very long for a handgun, and his wounded arm made his aim unsteady. He fired three quick rounds.

The sniper flung himself behind a tree. The Desert Eagle was a handgun, but it was a .50-caliber handgun, loaded with armor-piercing ammunition. The conical, Teflon-coated bullets were designed to penetrate Threat Level III ceramic armor plates.

A Newfoundland pine presented little obstacle.

Bark flew as Bolan emptied his pistol into the sniper's cover. The pistol racked open on empty, and he ejected his spent magazine. The sniper rose and began running through the trees. He had dropped his rifle, and he clutched his right arm to his chest.

Bolan slammed in a fresh clip and charged after him. The sniper disappeared as the land dipped. The soldier ran for all he was worth as he heard the sudden cough and snarl of a motorcycle. He ran up onto the rise in the tree line and saw the bike and its rider weaving through the trees. Bolan burned all seven rounds in his pistol, but the rider was already two hundred yards out and pulling away.

Bolan lowered his empty pistol as the sniper disappeared into the hills.

He walked to the tree he'd holed and found the sniper's rifle covered with blood. It was a very old-fashioned semiautomatic rifle with a telescopic sight. Bolan picked up the rifle by its sling and walked back to the corral. He looked back. Antonetti had seen his charge in her rearview mirror, and the Bronco was coming back. Bolan walked past the collapsed stable and examined the aftermath at the Dildo Corral.

The dead lay strewed in an arc around the corral entrance. Six bodies lay riddled with gunshot wounds. Bolan could clearly see the damage his pistols had done and the rifle wounds the sniper had inflicted on his own men to leave no witnesses.

Bolan turned at the sound of a hacking groan.

A man lay in the drainage ditch. His shotgun a few feet away. He had been shot in the shoulder, and from the ugly way it hung Bolan could tell both the collarbone and the shoulder blade behind it were shattered. The man was coughing. Bolan knelt beside him. He had seen the man's face in Antonetti's file. It was Jerome "The Jew" Siderisi. There was blood staining the wet gravel under Siderisi's head. It looked like his skull had taken a good bounce when he had fallen.

Siderisi feebly reached under his coat as he became aware of Bolan. The Executioner swatted his hand away and confiscated the small pistol the killer was carrying.

Bolan glanced back at the man in the middle of the corral with the knife in his throat. He had seen that man's face in the RCMP files as well.

"Hey." Bolan poked Siderisi in his good shoulder. "I killed your little buddy, Scotty."

"Fuck you." Anger focused The Jew's eyes slightly. "You're dead."

"Who's going to kill me?" Siderisi winced as Bolan unslung the bloodstained sniper rifle and tossed into his lap. "Your sniper friend?"

Siderisi stared at the weapon in shock. "Carlo."

"I took out your best. I took The Wolf. I took Scott Clylan. I took Carlo. You got nothing left."

Siderisi spit at Bolan and missed. "You got Big Damage coming down your ass."

"Oh yeah? Who's gonna do me big damage?"

"Big Damage is gonna—!" Siderisi's eyes flared, and his jaw clamped shut.

Bolan nodded. Big damage was not an event. It sounded like "Big Damage" was somebody's name.

The Executioner stood.

"You're dead!" Siderisi screamed. "You're fucking dead!"

"Yeah, yeah, yeah." Bolan nodded. "You just lay there and bleed awhile."

Antonetti came over and surveyed the scene. "What's his problem?"

Bolan glared at the killer. "Jerome's got a concussion and can't keep his mouth shut."

Siderisi turned white with rage.

Bolan nodded at him knowingly. "When you take him into custody in St. John's, spread the word that he gave up Carlo and Big Damage. We'll see what that does to his life insurance premiums."

"Motherfucker! You're dead! You hear me! You and the Mountie bitch! We got holes dug for your asses! You understand!" Spittle flecked Siderisi's lips as he screamed at the sky. "Look at me! I'm talking to a ghost! Fucking ghosts!"

Bolan ignored his ranting. "How's Kubak?"

"I bound up his arm. He lost a lot of blood. We need to get him looked at. You, too." She stared down at the screaming gangster in the ditch. "Who's Big Damage?"

"I don't know. But we're about to find out."

7

"What have you got for me, Bear?"

Aaron Kurtzman's face was grim. "Not much," he said, shaking his head.

Bolan sat at the table drinking coffee. The buckshot pellet had ripped a furrow in his arm that had taken fourteen stitches to close. His armor had stopped everything else. Dr. Ferentinos had confirmed that neither he, Antonetti nor Kubak were infected with the mutant bacteria. Bolan still felt like a mule had trampled him. "Anything on Big Damage?"

"I don't know, Striker. Sounds like slang to me."

"I got the impression that it's a person rather than an activity."

"Okay, so we assume its some guy's nickname. It's still slender as hell."

"I know, but Siderisi clammed up real quick after he let it slip. I get the feeling Big Damage is a step up the ladder. If he's Union Corse, then someone in the U.S., Canada, France or a French possession has got to have a rap sheet on him with his aliases."

"I'll put Akira on it."

"What'd you'd come up with on the rifle we recovered in Dildo?"

"We ran a full battery of tests on it. There were no fingerprints. The weapon was French." Kurtzman brought up a photo of the rifle on the screen.

"The serial numbers had been ground off, but we used a muriatic acid bath and ran an X-ray. We recovered the ghost of the strike marks. According to the serial number, it was French Foreign Legion issue."

That was interesting. Bolan had gone up against and cooperated with the Legion before. "Bear, the French Foreign Legion keeps very tight control on their weapons, and they never throw anything away. Their surplus stuff just doesn't make it onto the black market."

"You think this guy is a Legion veteran?" Kurtzman asked.

"Whoever he is, he took a running target at two hundred yards. Then he extracted. He was good. Get anything you can on the name Carlo and the Legion's past sniper specialists. Get the whole team working."

"I'm on it," Kurtzman replied.

"You have anything on the Prettys or their cousin Sylvan's activities in Cape Breton?"

"That's the one good lead we do have. All three of them worked at the Skir Dhu Distillery. Located in the town of Skir Dhu, Cape Breton."

For the second time the word distillery ran up a flag in Bolan's mind. "Wasn't there an incident in a distillery in Scotland a few years ago?"

"You know, that does sound familiar." Kurtzman's hands flew across his keyboard. "Yeah, there was an incident. A distillery's security cameras picked up some people in dark clothing prowling around inside the distillery after hours. The woman monitoring the security cameras sounded the silent alarm. When the police arrived, the individuals had vanished without a trace."

"They extracted."

"That's the theory. There was a minor stink about it. The English papers ran some inflammatory stories. There were two schools of thought. One was that they were CIA operatives, or else they were agents of MI-5."

"Why would Western intelligence agencies be sending agents into Scottish whiskey distilleries in the dead of night?"

Kurtzman read the report. "The newspapers thought they might be searching for chemical or biological weapons."

Bolan nodded.

"Distilling whiskey is a biological process. You have fermentation chambers, cold rooms and storage areas on the premises. If you had the facility, converting it would not be that difficult. Assuming you have total control over your workforce, and we'll assume the Union Corse is hiring only insiders, and they actually put out some whiskey once in a while, it would be a hard act to detect. Plus, if the distillery bottles in any quantity, then you would have legitimate air, land and sea distribution channels already in place. Bear, I need a list of everyone who has any controlling interest in the Skir Dhu Distillery."

"Okay."

"My best guess is that the distillery was originally a Mafia money laundering outfit. Then someone, somewhere got the bright shining idea and it was converted."

"Not bad, I—"

"I need a list of every whiskey distillery in Canada and their distribution routes, locally and worldwide."

"I'm on it." Kurtzman raised a knowing eyebrow. "You're heading to Cape Breton Island?"

"Yeah, with as many RCMP Emergency Response Teams as I can requisition."

Cape Breton

THE RCMP SWEPT down from the sky. Local police and RCMP units had the distillery cordoned off while Cape Breton fire units worked. Huge plumes of black smoke were rising up like columns into the sky.

The Skir Dhu Distillery was burning out of control.

The helicopters landed, and the Emergency Response Teams deployed in black raid suits, gas masks and wielding German Heckler & Koch submachine guns.

The fire chief removed his helmet and scratched his head as Bolan, Antonetti and Dr. Ferentinos approached. "Uh…something I should know?" he asked.

Dr. Ferentinos showed him his CDC badge. "Chief, you're aware of the situation in Newfoundland?"

"Jesus, yeah, that flesh-eating shit?"

"Yes." The doctor nodded tolerantly. "We have reason to believe that the outbreak may have originated here."

The chief turned pale.

"Your men should be fine fighting the fire. Make sure they're wearing masks and gloves. Make sure they don't touch anything. The fires have probably done the vast majority of the decontamination for us."

Bolan lifted his head. "You smell that?"

"Yeah," the chief said. "Gasoline. A shitload of it. What the hell they were doing with that much gas in a distillery is beyond me."

Antonetti frowned. "Arson."

"Yeah, that's what I was thinking, too. I just didn't want to be the one to say it out loud," the chief said quietly.

"Why is that?"

He leaned in close. He put a finger to his nose and shoved it to one side. Bolan smiled thinly. The local fire chief knew the Union Corse had its fingers in the Skir Dhu distillery.

"Yeah, gas," Bolan acknowledged. "What else do you smell?"

"Well, we got gasoline, whiskey, and—" The chief lifted his head up. "Jesus, what the hell is that? It's—"

"It's sulfuric acid," Bolan said.

"Goddamn it, you're right! Listen, I gotta go tell my men we have a HAZMAT situation."

The chief ran forward to the lines of firemen.

Bolan turned to Ferentinos. "You're the expert. Would sulfuric acid do the job?"

"Well, yes. After all, we're talking about a bacteria that hosts in living organisms. You bathe it in sulfuric acid, you not only kill it, but it's gone, dissolved. If that's what they flooded their specimen and maturation tanks with, I doubt whether there will be any useful biological evidence that can be extracted. That's not even including the effects of the building fire."

Antonetti watched the distillery burn to the ground. "So we're out of leads," she said.

"No, we just start from the bottom again. We find out what family had controlling interest in the distillery. Then we do a hard probe and move up the ladder. Starting with the errand boys if we have to," Bolan said.

"Hard probe? My superiors are all ready having problems with your methods. If you break any more Canadian laws—"

"I'm prepared to break every law Canada has on the books." The Executioner didn't blink. "And I'm prepared to accept the consequences of my actions."

"Goddamn it…" Antonetti stormed away and furiously began punching numbers into her cell phone.

Dr. Ferentinos looked at Bolan with wonder.

"You're holding up pretty well for a guy who got shot three days ago," Bolan said.

"Yeah, well." Ferentinos grinned. "I work out."

Bolan took out his cell phone and punched a number. A machine answered and the soldier typed in the current code. Kurtzman picked up on the first ring. "Striker, I—"

"Bear, the situation is starting to unwind. My relationship with the RCMP is being strained to the breaking point. I need a solid lead to show them, and I need it now."

"Well, I'm glad you called. I was just about to call you."

"What have you got?"

"I've got Big Damage."

8

Big Damage sat enthroned as the "beautiful people" of Montreal writhed against one another to the pulsing rave rhythm. The music throbbed at earsplitting decibels, and neon lights flashed. Le Club 4 was one of the most exclusive clubs in the city. The bouncers decided who was given or denied entry based on fame or looks. Besides the athletes, actors and glitterati of two continents, there was another kind of people known to frequent the club.

Dangerous people.

The Executioner had cut to the front of the line and looked into the bouncer's eyes over the rims of his sunglasses and smiled. The doorman had nodded and opened the rope for them without a word. Bolan was wearing around ten thousand dollars worth of immaculately tailored Italian silk, wool and leather.

Sergeant Antonetti was dressed like a prostitute. They leaned over the balcony and took it all in.

Big Damage reclined in splendor in the VIP area. A pair of platinum blondes that personified the dizzying zenith of cosmetic surgical augmentation flanked him.

Bolan compared the man on the blue velvet couch to the file he had read. At six foot one, Bruno "Big

Damage" Sedin was not particularly gigantic for a wrestling superstar, but his broad shoulders and tiny waist coupled with his immense muscular development gave him the physique of a comic-book superhero. His biceps were his trademark. At twenty-two and a half inches they were out of all proportion to his already massive development. He'd had a million nicknames for them, "The Twin Peaks," "The Guns of Navarone," but had finally settled on "The Hawthorns." No one had known what it meant, but thousands of rabid fans had chanted for the Hawthorns in packed arenas throughout North America. When the Hawthorns flexed, "Big Damage" was imminent.

Bruno Sedin no longer sported bleached platinum hair, and he wasn't wearing tie-dyed wrestling trunks and feather boas, but his engorged arms looked inhuman draped across the top of the couch, and his chest strained the blue silk of his sleeveless shirt. Big Damage might have been retired, but Bolan could see he was still in heavy training and still abusing muscle-enhancing pharmaceuticals.

Bolan had done some research on Sedin on the flight from Nova Scotia. Sedin's pro wrestling role was always that of the bad guy. The only thing bigger than his biceps was his personality. He could have a crowd roaring for his blood seconds after entering the ring, and he had risen to the heights of his profession.

Big Damage also developed a certain reputation.

He liked to hurt people, including other wrestlers who he thought had crossed him or stolen his spotlight. Athletes of much larger stature didn't want to get in the ring with him. His staged submission holds could turn brutally real in an instant, and he was not afraid of changing the prearranged choreography. Whispers of connections to organized crime dogged him. Before becoming a wrestler, he was rumored to have been a leg-breaker for the Mob in Montreal. In the late 1990s, at the height of his fame, he had been arrested in connection with a steroid distribution network that had encompassed nearly all of Canadian professional sports. Mob financing was spoken of but not proved. He'd also picked up some very expensive recreational drug habits. Sedin had avoided real jail time and had done only two years in a correctional country club. When he got out, the enemies he had made in the wrestling world and his tarnished public reputation had left him effectively barred from the ring.

Big Damage wasn't going to go back to wrestling in high-school gymnasiums or breaking thumbs in back alleys. He was still a cult figure. Sedin knew a lot of famous people and had a lot of connections. He was a very dangerous man, and whatever it was he was currently doing for the French Mafia, the glorious results of it pulsed and glowed in three stories of hip-grinding decadence.

Somehow, Big Damage was connected to the bacteria that had the entire province of Newfoundland under quarantine.

Antonetti leaned in and whispered in Bolan's ear. "How do you want to play it?"

The RCMP sergeant's minuscule top and skintight pants struggled to keep her charms contained. Her discomfort with the outfit made her look like a farm girl gone bad in the big city.

"How about I pick a fight?" Bolan suggested.

Antonetti stared over at the VIP lounge. "You want to pick a fight? With him?"

Bolan shrugged. "Sure."

"I'll light you a candle."

"Just back me up if it comes to gunplay," Bolan said as he took Antonetti's hand. They made their way down from the balcony and waded across the crowded dance floor. They mounted the red carpet leading up to the VIP dais. At the top of the steps, a pair of bouncers barred their way.

"I just flew in from Newfoundland." Bolan spoke loud enough to be heard on the dais. "I got something for the big man."

"Let him through," Big Damage said before the bouncers could react.

Bolan and Antonetti stepped into the VIP area. Beyond the balcony were several doors where more private VIP activities took place. Big Damage regarded Bolan and Antonetti with a deceptively lazy smile. He reached out to either side and stretched the Hawthorns. His sinews creaked and popped like an iceberg about to give way. He relaxed again with a sigh and gathered his women against him. They snuggled happily into his physique. "You flew in from the Rock?"

"Just today."

"Man, I hear people's flesh is bubbling off their bones over there." Sedin cocked his head slightly. "And I don't like Newfoundland, even on a good day. Nothing but fucking Newfies there, man."

The bouncers laughed.

"Yeah." Bolan nodded. "But I brought you something."

"Oh, yeah?" Sedin smiled. "I like presents."

The Executioner opened his coat to reveal a pair of nickel plated Manurhin .357 Magnum revolvers. The bouncers took a step forward as Bolan dropped the weapons with a clatter onto the low table before Sedin. Big Damage's vague smile remained fixed on his face as he waved off his goons.

"Oh, look. Guns. I'm sorry, Officer, but I'm on parole, and I firmly support the *Firearms Act*. I'm afraid I can't accept those."

"They belonged to Scott Clylan," Bolan said. "He doesn't need them anymore."

Sedin's smile widened. "Who?"

Bolan reached behind his back and drew a .32 Falcon pistol and tossed it onto the growing pile of iron. "That one belongs to The Jew. He's in custody. On the Rock. Spilling his guts." The Executioner matched Sedin's knowing smile. "That's how I found you."

Sedin's face froze for a split second. His women looked back and forth between Big Damage and Bolan in vague fear and confusion.

"Well, now." Sedin's smile returned. "You know something? I don't think you're a cop." He took his time running his eyes up and down Antonetti. "Now her? She's a cop. She blushes real nice, right down to those tits of hers, and they've spent more time in body armor than bustiers. She can barely walk in those heels."

Antonetti glared.

Big Damage turned his attention back to Bolan. "But you? You're a fucking American. I don't know what you're doing here, but somehow I don't think you have any jurisdiction." Sedin shook his head in amusement. "You know, I got security cameras observing this little encounter. I got you throwing guns around, and Tits here hasn't flashed a badge yet." Sedin jerked his head at the bouncers. "Rog, rip his fucking arms off. Mark, toss the bitch off the balcony."

The bouncer moved.

"Stop!" Antonetti shouted. "RCMP—"

Bolan felt a hand slap down on his shoulder. He grabbed the hand and the wrist behind it and dropped to one knee, torqueing his torso in a perfectly executed shoulder throw. The women screamed and cringed against Sedin as the bouncer sailed over them and smashed through one of the opaque glass doors. In the private room, an orgy of interlocked naked bodies broke apart and joined in the screaming. Bolan rose and turned.

Mark held Antonetti overhead, prepared to do his boss's bidding. Bolan beckoned the big man. "Hey. You. Come here."

The man dropped Antonetti like a sack of potatoes and moved in with a grace that belied his size. His slow-eye swiveled onto Bolan with sudden, disturbing binocular intensity. He spoke jovially. "Gonna fuck you up, lad."

His spatulate hands reached out to rend Bolan limb from limb.

Bolan's fist blurred between them. The second joint of his middle finger protruded into a one-knuckle fist that cracked between the bouncer's nose and upper lip. Bolan's second blow was exactly the same except it sank into the notch between the collarbones and crushed his trachea. The third blow turned into a right hand lead that landed against the man's jaw like a train wreck.

The man's eyes rolled as he toppled to the carpet like a felled tree.

"Marcel! Tino!" Sedin hadn't moved. "Little help up here!"

A black man in a Montreal Alouettes jersey came bounding up the stairs. His fist cocked back as he charged full tilt to the landing.

Antonetti stuck out her foot and Marcel went forehead first through the table and lay unmoving.

Tino lumbered up to the landing and stopped, unsure of what to do about the intruder. "Yo, Big D. You want me to, uh…" He trailed off uncertainly.

"Naw. Don't worry about it, Tino." Sedin still sat on the couch unconcerned. "Call the cops."

Antonetti rose painfully. A remarkable bruise already blackening her shin. "I am the cops."

"I know." Sedin smiled. "I want to file a complaint against you."

Tino appeared relieved. He produced a cell phone and began tapping numbers.

Sedin never took his eyes off Bolan. "You know something, tough guy? Sometime soon." Big Damage popped his biceps. "Me. You. The Hawthorns. We're gonna get together and have ourselves a real, good old-fashioned Come to Jesus."

9

"What have you got?" Bolan asked over the secure line.

"Not much. We already gave you all we had on Sedin," Aaron Kurtzman replied.

"But you have something, Bear. Or you wouldn't have called."

"We hacked the French Foreign Legion database."

"And?"

"That didn't bring up anything concrete, but we ran the name, Carlo. There were a bunch of them, so we tied that in with everything the FBI, CIA and Interpol had on Union Corse activities."

"You have a name?"

"We have a ghost."

Bolan had faced ghosts before. "You're saying our boy is officially dead."

"Supposedly. The trail we found goes like this. We have a man by the name of Chavel MalCroix, born in Corsica, a genuine relation of Napoleon. Also a member of the Union Corse in long standing. He was one of their hit men. Very active in Paris. Loved the highlife. Expensive dresser. Member of high society and feared by every lowlife in Paris. He was a genuine James Bond licensed to kill kind of guy, except he was working for the French Mob. He was unsuccessfully implicated in fourteen killings and a suspect in a number of others. Almost all of the victims were government witnesses or jurors in Union Corse trials. He was a fixer."

"So what happened?"

"MalCroix was finally arrested and convicted of the murder of a Parisian high justice who was overseeing the trial of a Union Corse capo. But MalCroix escaped right from the maximum security wing. In the process, he killed two guards with his bare hands, and once he made it out of the inner compound he simply disappeared without a trace."

"So." Bolan saw where this was going. "How was recruiting that year for the Legion?"

"That same year, according to the Legion records Akira hacked, a man matching the age and description of Chavel MalCroix joined the Legion claiming Belgian citizenship, and yes, he is on your list of Legion sniper specialists. Six confirmed kills in the first Gulf war serving with the parachute commandos."

"So he's got his jump wings."

"And in his spare time he qualified as a Legion hand to hand combat instructor."

"What's his name?"

"Carlo Ettiene."

Bolan nodded to himself slowly. Mob hit men were one thing, Special Forces commandos were another, and the next time Carlo came, he wouldn't be an insurance policy for Newfoundland thugs.

Ettiene would come in up close and personal.

"Another thing. Rumor is, during his stint in the Legion, Ettiene also specialized in interrogation techniques."

Bolan knew the French had always played rough in that department. "So what happened to him?"

"He disappeared, AWOL, out of the blue. Never been seen since."

"So other than the rifle, how do we tie him in with what's happening now?"

"There is an Interpol report that says the Union Corse has a hit man known only as Carlo, never been caught, never been seen, no description, and rumored to have had several plastic surgeries. He's supposed to be their ultimate fixer in Europe. He makes a kill and then disappears to Canada until he's needed again. The two French mobsters who gave up that tidbit to Interpol are both dead, killed with a high-caliber rifle from a distance."

All of this was fascinating, but it told Bolan nothing except that he had a serious problem on his trail.

He was going to have to force some issues. "I'm going to need the names of the number one mobsters in Quebec."

Kurtzman read Bolan's mind. "You're going to keep going rolling thunder until these guys come out from under their rocks."

Bolan agreed. "But if I had to bet, they're already on the move."

"You think they're going to bug out?" Kurtzman asked.

"No, I think they're going on the warpath."

Quebec City

IT WAS A FULL meeting of the board.

The Boss lit himself a cigarette. "So, who is this asshole?"

Carlo Ettiene flexed his forearm, feeling the stitches tighten as his muscles contracted. "He's no regular cop."

Big Damage was sprawled out in an overstuffed leather chair. "He took out Rog and Mark without blinking. I looked in his eyes. He's a real son of a bitch. He had Tino shitting his shorts. Had to give him a bye, or I think the man would have destroyed the club."

The Moor's long black hair fell forward as he tilted his head and smiled. "I notice you didn't lend a hand."

Sedin shrugged carelessly. "I wanted to see what he could do."

The Boss raised an eyebrow. "And?"

"He reminded me of me." Sedin casually flexed his biceps. "Only smaller. I can take him."

"You know—" The Boss blew a smoke ring "—that's what Carlo said."

Carlo scowled.

"I'll send him back to the States for you, broken, blind and brain damaged," Sedin said.

"We need to set him up." The Moor leaned back in his chair. "We need to set him up for the big fall."

Carlo considered the man he had exchanged fire with on the Rock. "You know they say the best way to a man's heart is through his dick."

The men in the room laughed unpleasantly.

"You have something in mind?" The Boss asked.

"The American?" Carlo took a manila folder and slid it across the desk. "He's still a mystery, but the bitch—"

The Boss opened the folder and gazed at Sergeant

Daniela Antonetti's latest RCMP file. "Nice tits." He shook his head as he read. "Jesus, Carlo, she's from fucking Nunavut?"

"Yeah, but don't worry about that. It's gotta be coincidence."

Sedin smiled. "Don't let the snow-bunny looks fool you. She's the one who put Marcel's face through the table. Stuck out her leg and sent him flying. I couldn't have choreographed it better."

The Boss nodded. "I think we need an interview with this fucking Mountie."

The men in the room laughed again. They all knew what "interview" meant.

The Boss examined the picture of Antonetti. "The Spider likes blondes, and he loves big tits. And God knows he loves working with cops."

Laughter filled the warehouse.

The Boss lit another cigarette. "What's the story on The Jew?"

"He was going to be held without bail." Carlo steepled his fingers. "But we happen to have a piece of that Judge on the Rock. Bail was set at one hundred thousand." Carlo nodded at The Moor. "I sent the bill to your friends."

"They'll pay."

The Boss blew a smoke ring. "So where is he now?"

"I smuggled him off the Rock."

"Why isn't he here?"

"He was shot. The cops gave him medical treatment, but the trip home left him pretty banged up. I sent him to a doctor friend of ours. He's in Montreal. I'm putting him on a boat to France as soon as the doctor clears him for travel."

"Good." The Boss was pleased. Siderisi was a useful asset, and he didn't want to have him killed unless necessary. The Boss turned to The Moor. "You got that sick fuck Esau with you?"

The Moor and smiled. "He's right outside."

"Send him in."

The Moor clicked his pager and Esau Buriz came into the room with one hand beneath his coat. The Moor's right-hand man took his hand away from his shoulder-holstered 12.3 mm Russian revolver and looked at The Boss. "Yeah?"

The Boss turned Antonetti's file around and slid it across the desk. "This bitch is RCMP. I want you and the Spider to give her the full treatment."

Esau's smile grew wide enough to reveal his pierced tongue. "Oh yeah."

"One other thing."

"Yeah?"

"Videotape it." The Boss nodded. Esau and the Spider together were the things that nightmares were made of. "Then send a copy to the commissioner of the Royal Canadian Mounted Police. It's about time we taught those Mounties a lesson."

Carlo poured himself a whiskey. "Maybe Jerome would like to watch. He owes that bitch."

The Boss was delighted. "Yeah, let's see if Jerome's up for some audio visual entertainment.

Montreal

BOLAN BIT INTO HIS STEAK. One of the nice things about Canadians was that they knew a thing or two about beef. They also knew what rare meant. The Alberta-raised beef was two inches thick, spiced and seared to perfection on the outside, hot and bloody on the inside.

Antonetti was tearing into her prime rib like a starving she-wolf. "So what's next?" she asked.

"Sedin's the only real lead we have at the moment. We know he's part of this, but I've been going over his rap sheet, and I haven't found any connections I can recognize," Boland said.

"So what are you going to do? Sedin's already registered a complaint with the local RCMP detachment. He's pretty slick"

"Don't know. I guess I'm just going to have to lean on him."

Antonetti's eyes widened slightly. "You'd better be real careful how you do that, and I'm not talking about legalities. I looked in his eyes and he had too much..." She searched for a word.

"Control." Bolan finished the sentence.

"Yeah. You threw down the guns, let him know what you knew, you took out his muscle men and he just sat there, smiling."

Bolan had locked eyes with Sedin and seen a psychopath. Lines that normal human beings couldn't cross would mean nothing to him. Buttons you could press on others would be meaningless in his psyche. Normal methods of arrest, control and interrogation would fail, notwithstanding his superhuman physique. Once he went in motion the only thing that would stop him would be a bullet through the brain.

"He's a real specimen," Bolan said quietly.

"What about this Carlo Ettiene guy?"

"He tried to take us out once." Bolan had given her a file with everything that Kurtzmen had come up with. "I suspect he'll try again."

"So…" Antonetti smiled. "I'm going to tell my superiors the plan is to go pick another fight with a psycho who can bench-press five hundred pounds and we're going to let a trained special forces sniper take another shot at us?"

Bolan nodded. "Yup."

"Oh this is going to be good." Antonetti laughed. "A girl could pick up bad habits following you around."

Bolan put some cash on the table. "I'll walk you up."

They left the hotel restaurant. Antonetti waited for the elevator doors to close before speaking again. "So how are you going to make Sedin show his hand?"

"Piss him off."

"Uh-huh, and what about when Ettiene comes for us?"

"If I can force Sedin to make a mistake, maybe he'll give us a lead on Carlo."

They walked to Antonetti's door. She leaned against it looking up at Bolan.

Bolan smiled. "That's quite a posture you've adopted."

Antonetti blushed. "I can't let you in."

Bolan shrugged. "I didn't ask."

"I know, but I'm about to."

"I'm flattered."

"You push all the right buttons on a girl like me." Antonetti sighed wistfully. "So I think I'm going to have to say good night. We're working together, and we have a big day chasing flesh-eating bacteria tomorrow."

"Get some sleep. I'm going to contact my people. If they have anything interesting I'll call you," Bolan said.

ANTONETTI WATCHED BOLAN as he walked away, and then went into her room.

An arm snaked around her throat. Antonetti instinctively threw an elbow, but it struck an unyielding abdominal wall. She flung her other arm back gouging for an eye with her thumb. Her wrist was seized and yanked up under her chin with childlike ease. The gigantic arm curving beneath her chin flexed, and the massively peaked biceps popped and cut off her carotid artery on one side. Her own arm was pinned against her, cutting off the blood from the other side. Her free arm flailed awkwardly as her vision began to darken.

Sergeant Antonetti was in a Cobra Clutch.

Big Damage leaned his cheek against hers, eliminating the possibility of a backward head butt. "Hey, baby."

Antonetti tried to stamp the inside of Sedin's shin, but the man just laughed. The world began receding down a dark tunnel.

"Sweet dreams, Princess, 'cause when you wake up, it's nightmare time."

10

Bolan made a call. Hal Brognola answered immediately and the Man from Justice did not sound amused. "I just got a call a minute ago. Rumor has it you're off the reservation," he said.

"We've got an officer whose life is on the line. There's no time to go through procedures," Bolan replied.

"Yeah, and 'Rogue U.S. agent running amok in Canada' has a ring to it the State Department and newspapers will just love."

"I'm bringing Antonetti back, dead or alive, and I'm burning down the people who did it." Bolan explained that the RCMP were not cooperating with him anymore and had seized his weapons.

"Right." It was clear the big Fed had expected no less. "So what do you need from my end?"

"I need a name."

"What kind of name?"

"The biggest fish in Montreal."

"Striker, we don't even know which crime Family we're going after."

"I don't care, give me the biggest name. Top of the

food chain, and I'll work my way down to the bottom feeders who have Dani."

"Jesus, you're talking about a hard probe right in—"

"I'm talking search and destroy, Hal. Like you said, I'm off the reservation."

"Damn it, Striker, I—"

"I need a name."

There was a long pause on the line. "I'll put the Bear on it. He'll call you."

"Thanks, Hal." Bolan hung up and dialed another number. It rang a number of times before there was an answer.

"Hello, this is Dr. Ferentinos."

"Hello, Doctor."

"Jesus! Where are you? The RCMP was just here."

"You still have that gun I gave you?"

"Yes…" There was a very long pause. "Why?"

"Can you bring it to me?"

"Umm, can't the RCMP give you one?"

"I'm currently AWOL from the RCMP."

"Oh…right."

"You remember Sergeant Antonetti?"

"Of course," Ferentinos said.

"They've got her."

"Got her? Who's got her?"

"The same people who shot you. The same people who are developing the bacteria."

"Jesus…"

"Yeah, I need you. I need an extra pair of hands."

"I'm still in Cape Breton at the distillery site with the

forensics team and a couple of bio-warfare specialists, we're—"

"What've you found?"

"Well, it's like you thought. Someone flushed the distillery tanks with sulfuric acid and burned them clean of any residual biological material. According to the fire chief, they then opened the valves and poured out the acid all over the distillery. Then they brought in the gasoline and torched the place. Even after the fire was out, the HAZMAT team had to completely flush the whole place with water to make it safe for the investigators. We're still looking, but we haven't found a trace of the bacteria at the site, and between the fire, the acid, and the flood, the fire investigator and the RCMP are doubtful of finding much in the way of fingerprints or physical evidence."

Bolan had suspected as much. "How fast can you get here?"

"I'm right in the middle of—"

"You won't find anything within your purview in Cape Breton. You just said so yourself."

"Well, I suspect you're right, but how can I—"

"You're head of the biological investigating team. Requisition military or RCMP transport. Tell them it's an emergency. It's approximately six hundred miles between Montreal and Cape Breton. You should be able to make it in two hours under emergency war power."

"I—"

"That will give me some time to do the legwork on my end. Call me at this number when you touch down."

There was silence on the other end.

"Doctor, I need you. So does Dani."

Ferentinos hesitated only a moment. "I'm on my way."

11

"So, I'm a wheelman now." Dr. Ferentinos regarded Bolan in grim amusement.

"Wheelman, backup, cavalry and conscience." Bolan measured the doctor. "If you aren't down for this, you'd better speak up right now."

"Oh, I'm…down, all right." Ferentinos sat behind the wheel of the rented Lincoln Aviator. He took out the snub-nosed 9 mm revolver. "You want it now?"

"No, you hold on to it."

"Why?"

"In case something goes wrong."

"What could go wrong?"

"If someone comes out besides me, get out of here. If they have guns or try and stop you, run them down or shoot them."

"What about you?" Ferentinos shook his head. "What are you going to do?"

"I'll probably pick up some guns inside."

"From whom?"

"From people who won't need them anymore. Keep the engine running."

Bolan slid out of the SUV and crossed the street to

Napoleon's Billiards. Napoleon's was nearly empty save for a few people who seemed more interested in smoking cigarettes and drinking beer than playing pool. Bolan walked straight to the back office. A fat man in a jogging suit sat with his chair leaning against the wall smoking a cigar. Bolan walked right up.

The fat man glared up from the sports section. His smoldering cigar stub hung from his lip as if it were stapled in place. "Who the fuck are—"

Bolan kicked his chair out from under him.

The fat man fell to the floor. "Shit!"

Bolan stepped on the mobster's face. Not hard enough to fracture his skull but hard enough to break his nose and drive the cigar into the back of his mouth. The hardman gagged and screamed, spitting blood, ashes and sparks as Bolan stepped over him and kicked in the office door.

Two men looked up from the game of cards they were playing across the office desk. The bald, skinny one with a fat belly looked past Bolan at the fallen muscle flailing on the floor outside.

"I don't know who you think you are!" the man snarled. "But you are fucking dead!"

"Guns," Bolan said.

"Guns? What fucking guns? Who the hell—"

Bolan slapped him. He used only the knob of bone at the bottom outside edge of his palm. The Executioner connected with his opponent's jaw half an inch below his left ear.

Georgie Gilasenti's jaw unhinged from his face with an audible pop. The gangster fell to his knees, clutching his face.

Bolan nodded at Georgie's brother Roman. "I need guns."

"I don't keep any fucking guns on the—" Roman backed up until his rear hit the back wall as Bolan came on. "Christ! Shit! Fuck! Yeah! Guns! You want guns? No fuckin' problem! All the fucking guns you want!"

Bolan seized Roman's wrist and turned it until the man's middle and ring fingers dug into his ulnar nerve. "Where?"

"The storeroom! The storeroom!" Roman's face contorted with pain.

"Let's go."

Two of the men who had been playing pool stood by the door. They held their pool cues in their hands. Bolan squeezed harder. "Tell them to back off," he ordered.

"Jesus! Fuck! Back off!"

The two men backed away.

"Is anyone in this place heavy?"

"Are you fucking nuts?"

"Where?" Bolan squeezed again. "The door behind the bar?"

"Yeah! Storage!" Roman shrieked. "Fucking storage!"

The fat man was starting to rise. He held his bloody nose and mumbled through burned lips. "You moth—"

Bolan kicked him in the face again, and this time he put his weight behind it. The blow stood the fat man up and dropped him back down again. He lay on the ground bleeding and weakly moving his arms and legs like an overturned turtle.

Bolan marched Roman to the storage room behind the bar and kicked the door. "Where?"

"There! In the crates! They came in today!"

Bolan put his foot behind Roman's knee and shoved.

The mobster fell to his hands and knees on the floor. He started to turn around. "Listen, there's been some kinda—"

Bolan put his foot into his chest and shoved harder. "Sit!"

Roman bounced against the wall and sat still.

Bolan clicked open his folding knife and pried open the lid of one of the crates. Inside were four Chinese AK-47 rifles packed in straw. "Ammo?"

"They're loaded! What the fuck? You want…" Roman trailed off in terror as Bolan turned his attention on him. "They came loaded."

Bolan checked the loads in one of the rifles. There were three crates of weapons. He took two of the assault rifles and stripped the rest of their magazines. Roman sat rubbing his wrist and sniffling. "You're not gonna kill me, are you?"

Bolan regarded Roman without blinking.

"Aw fucking shit man, you don't have to, you don't have to—"

Bolan drove the steel buttplate of his commandeered rifle between Roman's eyes, and the man slumped to the floor. The soldier stepped out of the storage room to find himself facing a phalanx of six men with pool cues. He noticed the fat man, rather remarkably, was back on his feet and holding a bar stool with both hands.

Bolan knew most of the people in Napoleon's were probably lowlifes, but they weren't all gangsters. They were just in the wrong place at the wrong time.

The rifle's 12-inch folding bayonet made an ugly clack as Bolan snapped it into place.

The fat man tossed away the bar stool and pointed accusingly at Bolan even as he backed up. "You're fucking nuts! You know that?"

The patrons of Napoleon's parted like the Red Sea as Bolan passed through them. He quickly crossed the street and tossed the rifles and his jacket full of spare magazines into the back seat of the vehicle. Ferentinos stared at the weapons. "So you ripped them off."

"Yeah." Bolan nodded.

"But…" Ferentinos frowned. "Now they know we're coming."

Bolan climbed into the passenger seat. "Who knows we're coming?"

"Who? You know, like, the French Mafia?"

"No." Bolan shook his head. "They have no idea what's about to hit them."

"Well…" Ferentinos pointed at Napoleon's. "What about them?"

Bolan shrugged. "They're Italian Mafia."

"So…you ripped off the wops to hit the frogs?"

"Yeah, pretty much." Bolan raised an eyebrow. "You got a problem with that?"

"Me? Hell no. I'm Greek." Ferentinos shrugged his good shoulder. "So we go hit the French?"

"No. We hit the Italians."

Ferentinos shook his head.

THE LINCOLN SLID to a stop. Bolan looked across the street at the low stone manor. It was built like a medieval fortress. It might well have had to withstand attacks by woodland Indians, Colonial American irregulars and even British Redcoats throughout its history. Despite its ancient construction, it appeared to have all the modern amenities, including a pair of goons in suits and sunglasses standing around outside the gate.

The Italian and French Mobs had both existed for a very long time in Canada. Sometimes cooperating, sometimes at war, most of the time in confrontation avoiding competition. The Italians had a lock on gambling and a great deal of the organized prostitution. The French ran most of the guns and drugs. They constantly jockeyed for territory. Things were currently on peaceful but unfriendly terms.

Bolan examined the forbidding stone structure again. "Wait here."

"Yeah." The doctor sighed. "I'll keep the engine running."

It was a beautiful, late-afternoon summer day, and Bolan's raincoat looked rather incongruous, but it was the only way to conceal a pair of assault rifles. The executioner slipped out of the car and crossed the street. One rifle was slung over his left shoulder, and he held the other pinched between his right arm and his ribs. He walked down the tree-lined boulevard and up to the gate. He put a bit of a stagger into his walk as he approached.

"Spare some change?" Bolan slurred his words.

One of the guards stepped forward. "Get the fuck out of here before I—"

Bolan opened his coat. He lifted his right elbow and the pistol grip of the AK-7 fell into his hand. He swung the rifle up and clipped the guard under the chin with the front sight. He brought the barrel crashing back down again and split open his forehead. The rifle-whipped goon fell senseless to the cobblestones.

The second goon stared frozen in shock.

Bolan reversed the rifle in his hands, grabbing it by the barrel and raising it like a baseball bat. The guard put up his hands to block, and Bolan dropped and shattered the rifle's stock across the man's knees. The guard screamed and collapsed in a heap. Bolan kicked him in the temple to shut him up. He relieved the two unconscious guards of their handguns and stripped his broken rifle of its loaded magazine.

The executioner took three running steps, vaulted himself over the iron gate and walked up the drive. The front door was massive, ironbound oak. The castlelike integrity of the ancient strong house had been compromised by a massive window that opened onto the front patio. Bolan grabbed a wrought-iron patio chair and hurled it through the glass.

Women inside began screaming.

Bolan entered the fortress of Gino Malatesta, the Don of Montreal. He walked into the massive kitchen. The evening meal was being prepared, and the kitchen smelled enticingly of old Italy. Two women went white as Bolan came in. They gasped in unison as they took in gulps of air for fresh screaming. Bolan held up his rifle and put a finger to his lips. The women's jaws clicked shut. He pointed his finger at the tile floor and they dropped like stones.

The enemy didn't know yet what was happening, and

Bolan wanted to keep it that way as long as possible. He took up a twelve-quart stockpot as a well-tanned man in a suit ran into the room, cell phone in his hand. Bolan flung the simmering soup onto the mobster like a medieval Frenchman hurling boiling oil onto the besieging English. The man shrieked and fell to the floor flailing and blistering.

Bolan knocked the man unconscious and walked on. He didn't have time to sweep the whole house. The Malatesta Family was not on a war footing, and cracking their castle had been fairly simple. This part of the mission was fact-finding, and Bolan was prepared to be merciful. He marched up the stairs.

"What's happening?" a man screamed from just out of sight. "What's happening?"

"Assassins!" Bolan shouted. "Assassins!"

The man ran onto the landing in a crouch holding a pistol.

Bolan slammed the barrel of his AK-47 across the bodyguard's wrist. The guard howled as his bones cracked. The pistol fell to the ground, and the soldier clamped his hand around the guard's throat. He walked him to the railing and helped him over the side. The man fell screaming and smashed through a coffee table below.

Bolan marched down the hall. A half-dressed man burst from a bedroom with a woman screaming somewhere behind him. The AK-47 barked twice in Bolan's hands, and the man staggered and fell with a bullet through both thighs.

Bolan swung up the hinged bayonet and snapped it into place as he moved on. He put his foot into the door of the study.

An old man in a wheelchair was fumbling through his desk drawer. Bolan strode across the room as Gino Malatesta brought up a small nickel-plated revolver with a shaking hand. Bolan lunged with his bayonet.

Gino winced and cried out as Bolan pierced his shoulder. He dropped the little revolver.

"I need information," Bolan said.

The old man whimpered feeble curses in Italian.

He ceased as the Executioner pressed the point of the bayonet into the hollow of his throat. Bolan tilted the muzzle toward the Don's eyebrows and spoke for the benefit of the person standing behind him.

"One move, and I open his head to the sky." The selector switch of the AK-47 made an ugly sound as Bolan flicked it to full-auto for emphasis.

The woman's voice was a husky snarl. "Leave him alone!"

Bolan kept the bayonet pressed into the hollow of Malatesta's throat as he turned to regard the Don's daughter.

Consolata Malatesta had looked gorgeous in the surveillance photos, but they had failed to do her olive-skinned beauty justice. She stood in a cotton sundress, her gray eyes full of rage. Black hair cascaded across her shoulders. Her ruby red lips were pulled back from her white teeth in a snarl. Forty years old and widowed, she was a force onto herself. She held a small Italian .380 pistol in both hands. Her breasts heaved with her rapid, shallow breathing but the weapon did not waver.

"Drop the gun," Bolan said.

The woman kept the gun pointed at Bolan's chest. She

was not trained enough to realize he was wearing body armor and to aim for the head.

"Drop the gun," Bolan repeated. "I could have killed your entire family. No one's dead, yet. I want information."

"You're not a cop."

Don Malatesta made a pathetic noise as Bolan leaned on the bayonet, and the skin of his throat dimpled inward. "I'm going to ask you one last time. Drop the gun, or I'll kill your father, and then I'll kill you."

The weapon fell to the floor.

"You're an American." Consolata's upper lip rose in distaste. "I don't know anything about the fucking Americans. We do not do business with them."

"I'm not interested in the U.S. Mafia Families at the moment."

The Don's daughter thrust out her jaw and lifted her chest in equal defiance. "Then what the fuck do you want?"

Bolan admired the view. "I want the Union Corse, here, in Montreal."

"The French Canadians?" Consolata blinked. "What about them?"

"An RCMP policewoman was kidnapped a few hours ago. Perhaps you heard that."

"I heard that," the woman conceded.

"The French have her. I want to know who would be carving the turkey and where they would be doing it."

"You come here? You torture my father?" The snarl returned to Consolata's mouth. "For that?"

"If I start asking Frenchmen, they'll know I'm coming." Bolan looked grim. "And I'll kill your father, you and your whole family to save her."

Wheels turned behind the fathomless gray eyes as they met Bolan's. "The French do not make turkeys, and certainly not of women."

"So what does the French Mafia in Montreal do with women they want to make an example out of?"

Consolata's eyes narrowed. "They make films."

"Where?"

"And what do I receive in return if I help you?"

"I won't burn down this house and everyone in it."

"That is not a very fair bargain."

"We're not bargaining." The Don whimpered as the parchment thin skin of his throat began to bleed beneath the Executioner's steel. "I'm taking."

Consolata's white teeth momentarily dug into the fullness of her lower lip. Gino Malatesta was the Don of Montreal, but he was old, wheelchair bound and was rumored not to be the man he once was. Other rumors whispered that more and more she was the real decision-making power behind the throne.

She drew herself up haughtily. "I will accept my father's life and the injury of my competitors as fair trade for the information, and the possible war it may bring with the Union Corse."

"When I'm done, there won't be any Union Corse left in this province." Bolan said. "Where?"

"I have heard rumors. And I can make a good guess." The gray eyes turned to ice. "But I will remember this, and I will remember you."

12

Daniela Antonetti sucked in a shuddering breath. During the long wait, part of her mind had held on to the irrational concept that this wasn't really happening. Even when they had begun setting up the cameras and the lighting, she had held out a bizarre belief that somehow things would be all right.

When The Jew had walked in and smiled at her, she had known with crystal clarity that she was dead, and that once they were done dead would be a blessing. Antonetti tried to steel herself for the absolute worst.

She spoke through clenched teeth. "You won't be arrested. You won't be tried. I'm not some fucking runaway no one's going to miss. No one is going to watch this and say it-was faked. I'm a decorated sergeant in the Royal Canadian Mounted Police. They will hunt you for the rest of your miserable fucking lives. The best you can pray for is that they shoot you when they find you. If you somehow survive to trial and incarceration, then individuals in the prison system, both guards and inmates, will be paid to visit shit on to you that makes this little room look like fucking Disney World."

"Fuck you!" The Jew shouted. "Your American friend is next!"

The twitchy camera assistant looked nervous as for the first time he realized just what they were doing and who they were doing it to. Esau Buriz and Spider Andrisenne laughed.

Buriz didn't say a word. Saliva dripped onto Antonetti as he bent down to put the prongs of the stun gun into her armpit.

The door flew off its hinges.

The AK-47 sounded like thunder in the enclosure of the soundproofed cell. The cameraman whipped around with his hand on his Colt .45 pistol, but 7.62 mm rifle rounds crushed his rib cage before he could clear leather. The Executioner swung his weapon on the men hovering over Antonetti and squeezed the trigger.

Spider Andrisenne yanked back, flailing as the 5-round burst blasted through his face.

Siderisi jumped to his feet with his pistol in his hand. He cursed as he recognized the American. The tiny pistol popped twice in his hand and he saw the bullets hit the American in the chest. The man didn't even flinch. The Jew raised his aim, but the shovel shaped muzzle of the AK-47 rifle swung around like God's own rod of correction. The fixed bayonet gleamed and was then occluded by orange fire. Jerome Siderisi's head blew apart in fluid fireworks as Bolan held his trigger down and the full-metal-jacketed onslaught hit like a hailstorm.

The AK-47 rifle clacked open on empty.

Esau Buriz charged in from the left screaming incoherently, the stun gun arcing in his hand.

Buriz rammed the stun-gun prongs into Bolan's shoulder, the soldier's body locking as the electricity spasmed through his body in a wave.

"Yeah! Yeah! Yeah!" Buriz punched the prongs into Bolan again and again as if the stun gun were a knife. He sank the prongs into the side of Bolan's neck.

Pulsing lights smeared behind Bolan's eyes. His legs turned into separate rubber entities he had no control over. The Executioner barely had the wherewithal to bring the bayonet blade between himself and Buriz. Metal grated on metal as Buriz shoved the double prongs against the quadrangular bayonet blade and hit the button. Bolan's hands locked around his rifle as 625,000 volts crawled through the weapon like lightning. Buriz cut the juice, and Bolan's hands twitched open. The AK-47 fell to the floor with a clatter.

Bolan's vision darkened.

Blood was pouring into his eyes. His tortured muscles shuddered uncontrollably as his will fought with his short-circuited nervous system.

Buriz leaped at Bolan, arms spread like a wrestler coming off the ring's top rope.

Bolan's twitching hand closed around the neck of a fallen tequila bottle. Glass shattered as he snapped the bottom against the concrete floor. The Executioner slammed the broken bottle underneath Esau's navel and ripped upward. Buriz gave a wheezing scream, and Bolan rammed his shoulder into the man's chest. Buriz staggered backward. His hands went to the gaping hole in his guts. His face registered shock as he tried to keep the ropes of his intestines from spilling out. He fell to the floor.

Bolan dropped the remnants of the tequila bottle and drew a shuddering breath. All of his opponents were down. He took the fallen switchblade and cut Antonetti's bonds. He sat on the bed, and she fell shuddering into his arms.

"You all right?" he asked.

"Goddamn it!" She made a choking noise and tears spilled down her face. Bolan took a leather jacket hanging on the wall and put it across her shoulders. He grabbed his phone.

"Doc, the room is clear. I need you. Bring your medical kit."

"Right, I'll be right in."

Bolan hung up and punched the buttons for the Montreal RCMP. "This is Matt Cooper. I have Sergeant Antonetti, she's alive."

The startled dispatcher began rapidly making who, what and where demands.

Dr. Ferentinos stepped into the room. He had a medical bag over his shoulder and held the 9 mm revolver Bolan had given him in his good hand. The doctor paled at the carnage and grimaced at what the scattered devices and paraphernalia implied. "Jesus…"

Sergeant Antonetti was lying on the bed. Her breathing was very shallow and rapid. She had gone into shock.

Ferentinos put his satchel on the bed and glanced at the phone. He could hear the shouts coming through the receiver. "Is that the RCMP?"

"Yeah." Bolan nodded.

"Why don't you let me handle this," he said.

Bolan handed Ferentinos the phone. "Thanks, Doc."

He had saved Antonetti, but he suspected he was still persona non grata with the Royal Canadian Mounted Police. They were going to blame him for putting her in this situation, and they might be right. Bolan suddenly felt a terrible need to sit down. He didn't, because he wasn't sure he would be able to get up again any time soon.

Ferentinos was juggling the phone between his shoulder and his jaw while he tried to prep a syringe one-handed. He frowned deeply at the blood pouring down Bolan's face, and peered into his eyes. He held up his hand. "How many fingers?"

"One."

"Do you know where you are?"

"Montreal, Old Port District."

Ferentinos cocked his head. "Who are you?"

Bolan's Arctic blue eyes stared at Ferentinos through a mask of coagulating blood. "I'm Batman."

Ferentinos sighed in defeat. "I had to try." He jerked his head toward the door. "Get the hell out of here. Take the car. Take your phone. Medics and the RCMP units are on the way. I'll have Antonetti stabilized in a few minutes. Call me when you get someplace safe. If I can, I'll come check on you or send someone I trust."

Bolan nodded, and even that tiny effort cost him.

The Executioner limped from the tiny corner of hell and out into the Canadian night.

13

Bolan lay on the bed with a bag of frozen peas on his face. He had managed to stave off the raccoon-mask bruising around his eyes, but he still had a very angry lump in the middle of his forehead. A screwdriver was slowly turning deeper and deeper into his brain behind his left eye.

The neon sign outside the window turned the motel room a gloomy coral color.

Bolan's phone was ringing on three lines.

He chose to answer the one that was the least likely to yell at him.

Antonetti's voice sounded strong over the phone. "How are you doing?"

"I have a headache."

"Oh fine, I don't let you into my hotel room, and now when I call you have a headache."

Bolan was relieved. If Antonetti still had her sense of humor, she was going to get past what she had gone through. "Well, you should have let me in."

"Don't I know it. Always sleep with the International Man of Mystery. Lesson learned."

"How are you?"

"I'm all right. They want to keep me today, and maybe tomorrow. Dr. Ferentinos has been an angel."

"And?"

"It could have been much, much worse…" Antonetti paused. "I have a lot to thank you for."

"Eat whatever they give you. Sleep if you can."

"The advice of a soldier."

"I'll visit you soon."

"I wouldn't if I were you. Your name is mud around here. If you show up here at the hospital or at RCMP Division headquarters, you will be detained."

Bolan heard an angry voice speaking in the background. "Is that him?"

"Gotta go." The line clicked dead as Antonetti hung up.

Bolan switched lines. "What have you got, Bear?"

"We've got Esau Buriz and Stefan "The Spider" Andrisenne."

"Tell me about The Spider."

"Andrisenne is a real lowlife. He's a Canadian citizen with definite connections to the Union Corse. He's also one of the top ten porn kings in Canada. He's been investigated for tax evasion a number of times but never convicted of anything. Rumor is he's involved in some very dark stuff."

"Rumors confirmed."

"He had a legit Internet porn kingdom, but no one could pin illegal stuff and make it stick until now."

"He blew it. He broke the rule."

"The rule?" Kurtzman was intrigued.

"Never get high on your own supply. Doesn't matter whether its drugs, porn or gambling. You run it and take the profits, but never participate. He dug what he was into way too much." Bolan's voice grew cold with the memory of what he had seen and experienced in the room beneath the Old Port District. "It got him into trouble."

"Well, you blew his head off, so he isn't going to be flipping for anyone in the near future."

"What about the other one, Esau? Any leads?"

"That's another story. Esau Buriz has dual French and Algerian citizenship. Real international character. Interpol has files on him. He's heavily into prostitution, and rumored to be big in the white slavery trade. Rumor is one hell of a lot of Eastern European girls who answer ads for modeling jobs or as mail-order brides for men in Western Europe and North America wind up in his hands, and I think you found out how a lot of them end up."

"What else?"

"The RCMP has multiple files on him. He's definitely Union Corse."

"People into that kind of vileness don't end up capos. I think he falls under the category of useful scumbag. Who's his higher up in the food chain?"

"That's where things get good. Prostitution and porn are huge earners, and according to RCMP files Buriz was paying his dues up to a genuine capo in the Canadian Union Corse."

"Give me a name."

"Gaultier Salamanca." Kurtzman's voice warmed with triumph. "Known as 'The Moor.'"

"Tell me about him."

"Half French, half Algerian, French citizenship, born on the Island of Corsica. Union Corse from the cradle, and, on his father's side, rumored to have ties with the North African branches of Islamic Jihad."

"He and Buriz must be related."

"Cousins."

Bolan smiled grimly. "Sounds like we just got a lead on why the Union Corse is messing around with biological weapons."

"That was my first thought as well. There's big money in terrorism if you play it right, and who the hell would suspect a whiskey distillery in Cape Breton as home of a flesh-eating bacteria bomb? It's nearly a perfect set up."

"It was, until they got careless. Speaking of which, my relationship with the RCMP is officially in the toilet."

"Oh, I know." Kurtzman's amusement was evident over the phone. "Hal's gotten an earful from his RCMP contact. Your name is mud."

"I'm going to need backup. I want Manning here, ASAP."

"That's going to go over like a French kiss at a family reunion."

"I need him. Carlo has upped the ante. So has the possibility of Islamic Jihad terrorists. My one friend in the RCMP is in the hospital, and the doctor is flapping on one wing. I need someone covering my six and Canada is Manning's stomping grounds."

"I'll see what I can do. I also have another possible lead."

"I'm taking whatever I can get right now."

"The CIA keeps tabs on Russian weapons scientists who have emigrated, particularly ones that have gone to places like the Middle East and North Korea."

Bolan saw what was coming. "How about the ones who have moved to Canada?"

"There are two that might interest you. Professor Grisha Jov and his wife, Dr. Kara Tamrynova."

"Let me guess, bacteriology is their specialty."

"Bacteriological warfare, to be exact."

BOLAN MADE READY to meet Gary Manning. It was 3:30 a.m., and they had a busy morning ahead of them. His head was still killing him. The bullet furrow in his arm ached with every move, but so far he felt no fever and the arm didn't look infected. He'd managed four hours of sleep. Upon awakening he'd found the uncontrollable tics and twitching from his repeated electrical shocks had subsided. He stared into the cracked and streaked bathroom mirror and saw a red-eyed punching bag staring back.

Bolan's phone rang, and he didn't recognize the number. "Hello?"

A woman's voice with a French accent answered. "Hello? Mr....Cooper?"

"Who's speaking?"

"This is Inspector Faith Gelinas, RCMP."

Bolan considered hanging up. The RCMP was one of the most modern police forces in the world, and it was in their power to intercept and trace cell phone calls. "How did you get this number?"

The inspector sounded vaguely offended. "How do you think?"

"Antonetti."

"That's right."

Bolan checked his watch. "What can I do for you, Inspector?"

"Well, it's more a question of what I can do for you."

"I thought my name was mud."

"Mud is an understatement. You are officially in a great deal of trouble, Mr. Cooper."

"So any assistance you can give me would be…unofficial?"

The inspector sighed. "Dani's a good friend of mine. We graduated cadet training together. I would have failed half of my exams without her help. I owe her a lot. She called me a few hours ago. She told me to…take care of you."

Bolan paused. It was nice to know he still had someone on his side. "Thanks."

"Yes, well. You made an impression, and you saved my best friend's life. Save this number. If you need something, or you're in real trouble, call me. I don't know what I can do for you. A get-out-of-jail-free card is above my pay grade, but if I can do something for you without jeopardizing my career, I will."

"I appreciate that, Inspector."

"Listen, Cooper. Officially? Your name is dogshit across the country. Unofficially? You've put some foot to ass on some real lowlifes, and you saved one of our own from a fate worse than death. You've got some people rooting for you."

"How's Dani holding up?"

"We talked for a while today. It could have been a lot worse, but she's a lot more traumatized by the ordeal than she'd like to admit. They're going to keep her for another day at the hospital. Then our people will probably want to give her a psychological evaluation."

"So she's off the case?"

"For the moment, pending doctor's clearance. Do me

a favor. Don't call her. At least not while she's in the hospital. You'll just get her in trouble. You can send her messages through me until they release her."

"Will do. How's Dr. Ferentinos?"

"He's AWOL. He went home to clean up before being debriefed, only he never got there." Inspector Gelinas laughed suspiciously. "You're saying he's not with you?"

Bolan glanced at his watch again. Dr. Ferentinos wouldn't be arriving for another fifteen minutes. "Nope. Not with me."

"Uh-huh. Listen, Cooper. I've got to get back to work. Let me know if I can do anything for you."

"I may need you to steal some files for me."

The woman sighed. "Yeah...I figured you'd say that. Listen, maybe we should meet. I'm on the bacteria case. I can bring you what I have. We can meet wherever you want."

Bolan considered the offer.

"You think I'm setting you up for an RCMP ambush?" she asked.

"No. Dani wouldn't have given you this number if she didn't trust you. We should meet later." Bolan checked the loads in Consolata Malatesta's pistol and tucked the little gun into his belt. "There's something I have to do first."

14

Gary Manning stared at the palatial estate clinging to the side of the mountain. The sun had not quite risen, and the walls of the estate were purple-gray in the pre-dawn. Bolan scanned the blueprints of the mansion. "So what else do we know about this guy?"

"According to Bear, he's the big French cheese." Manning checked the loads in his 10 mm Heckler & Koch submachine gun. An M-203 40 mm grenade launcher was attached beneath the weapon's barrel. "Top Union Corse man in Canada. The big boss man."

Bolan eyed the Interpol file photo. Serge Birkin was a remarkably ugly little man. His massive hooked and broken nose could be charitably described as "Gallic." He had big ears, big lips and squinty offset eyes. All of his features seemed too big for his head and were crowned by a thatch of hair that looked like it had been styled and then slept on. In the picture, smoke from his cigarette curled around his face as he stared into the camera with cold, unblinking hostility. Bolan nodded. The eyes said everything. Even without the corroborating FBI and RCMP files, Bolan could tell that Birkin was a stone cold dealer in human misery.

His right-hand man, Mano Razanjato was Algerian,

and wanted for questioning in France for terrorist related activities.

Bolan began hanging items onto his web belt from the bag Manning had brought. The big Canadian had brought the whole candy store with him.

Dr. Ferentinos watched the two warriors arm up. He'd spent the past two weeks on an island under military quarantine and surrounded by soldiers. These two men seemed to have more ordnance than the local police station. "You Americans sure have a lot of...guns."

Manning grinned. "I'm Canadian."

"Oh."

Manning's hand hovered over his bag. "You need a piece, Doc?"

"Uh, no, thanks. Your friend gave me one I still have, and with my bad shoulder I can't use a machine gun."

"Ah." Manning reached into the bag and pulled out what looked like a very large and violent-looking flashlight with a gaping muzzle rather than a lens. "HAFLA DM 34 hand-flame projector?"

"I'll take one." Bolan took the incendiary cartridge projector and thrust it into his belt.

The doctor had been fitted with a Threat Level III armored vest, a baseball cap with a bulletproof insert in the crown and a com link.

"Same drill, Doc. You're the wheelman." Bolan nodded up at the house. "Stay here. If we tell you to bug out, bug out. Don't wait for us. Anyone else but us comes out armed, bug out. If we find anything related to the bacteria, we'll call you in when it's clear. Got it?"

"Yeah." Ferentinos nodded. "I got it."

"I want you to know I appreciate what you're doing."

"It goes against every principle I have." The doctor took a long breath and let it out. "The guns, breaking the law, but I sat up all night with this gun you gave me, and I came to one inescapable conclusion. That bacteria cannot be allowed to be weaponized any further. The Hippocratic oath I took as a doctor demands that I take every action in my power to stop it."

Bolan nodded. He slung his weapon and took up a compound crossbow and a bag containing a coil of rappelling line. "Let's do it."

Bolan and Manning deployed. They wore black raid suits and were festooned with weapons, munitions and armor. This side of Mont Royal was fairly steep, and the mansions clung to its side supported by massive cables and struts, appearing to defy gravity from a distance. The two warriors made their way up through the trees. Birkin's mansion had walls in front and back and along one side. The side looking out over Montreal needed no security wall. The mountainside simply fell away, leaving the estate impregnable.

Impregnable to anything except specially trained warriors.

They clung to the hillside, crouched beneath the supporting structures of the terraced mansion. Manning reached into his gear bag and pulled out a crossbow bolt. He unfolded the three, foam-rubber-coated tungsten steel grappling hooks and locked them into place. He gave the bolt to Bolan. The Executioner attached the line to the base and laid the bolt in the guide.

The house had a series of steps up the mountainside,

a terrace garden, a vast patio above that, then the first, second and third stories. Manning stared up at the underside of the garden. "What do you think?"

"It's too quiet."

Manning consulted his watch. "It's five in the morning."

Bolan's instincts were speaking to him. "It's too quiet."

"You want to punt?"

"No." Bolan squeezed the crossbow's trigger. The grappling hook looped into the air and arced over the garden rail. The hook made almost no sound as its rubberized exterior hit the terrace. Bolan dragged it back until it hooked into the railing and the rope went taut. He gave it a tug and then pulled himself up hand over hand. Bolan stopped near the top and cinched his feet around the rope. He drew a small mirror on a telescoping rod and used it to peer around the terrace.

Manning whispered into his mike. "Anything?"

"No." The terrace contained a lawn with a fountain, and rows of small trees in massive earthen pots. Some garish statuary of the Greek gods reclined here and there around the garden in oversized, Olympian splendor.

Bolan slid over the rail and rolled behind a pot containing a flowering tree. "Clear."

Manning crawled up the rope like a spider and hopped over the rail. He crouched behind the potted tree opposite Bolan. Past the lawn a low brick wall surrounded the patio. Massive wooden deck furniture formed a loose arc around a stone barbecue large enough to feed a Roman Legion. The house above had the blinds drawn in all the windows.

"It's quiet," Manning said.

"Yeah."

"I'm going to the fountain." Manning rose into a crouch. "Damn!" He threw himself back behind cover.

Men with rifles had risen from behind the patio wall. The windows in all three stories of the house opened and stainless-steel rifle barrels glimmered in the pearly light of the dawn.

Armageddon erupted.

Automatic rifle fire rose in a deafening crescendo.

"Shit!" gummer Manning snarled.

Bolan silently agreed. They had walked into a trap, and it sounded like the entire Canadian army had come. Bolan flicked up his mirror and scanned quickly. There were at least two dozen hostiles, all armed with Ruger automatic carbines. Like amateurs, their stocks were folded, which was playing havoc with their aim. Their bursts were long as well, but they didn't seem to worry. Bolan could see the black drums on either side of the rifles of the closest gunmen.

Their rifles were equipped with 100-round assault C-Mags, and they were making up for accuracy and fire control with volume.

Bolan flinched as his mirror was shot off its extendable stalk. The hailstorm of lead went on and on.

"God...damn it!" Manning was busy replacing the tear gas grenade in his launcher with a frag from his belt. "Someone dropped a dime on us!"

Bolan hunched behind his pot and switched a new munition into his weapon as well. The clay pot shielding him cracked and broke and dirt spilled to the Spanish tile as his cover started to disintegrate. Consolata Malatesta came to his mind. "I think the Don's daughter may have gotten over her hatred of the French."

"Yeah, well maybe you shouldn't have poked her dad with a bayonet!" Manning suggested.

Bolan considered the hatred he'd seen in the depths of Consolata Malatesta's gray eyes. "You might be right."

Manning returned his attention to the matters at hand as leaves rained from the shuddering tree above him. "Frag 'em?"

"Frag 'em." Bolan flipped his submachine gun over the top of the pot and squeezed the M-203's trigger. Yellow flame belched, and Bolan's weapon wrenched in his hands with recoil.

Manning's weapon thumped a second later and the grenades detonated on the patio in a one-two punch, sending shrapnel hissing through the air in lethal spheres. The gunmen on the patio screamed as they were blasted and torn.

Bolan slid a fresh frag into his smoking breech and this time rose up from cover and aimed. His weapon thudded back against his shoulder and the grenade looped through the back patio door and detonated among the throng of firing riflemen.

Manning fired and decimated the group on the second-story balcony. They reloaded their launchers and the two warriors rose and advanced. The grenades had changed the trigger-happy attitudes of the rifleman. The survivors on the patio were running for the cover of the house. The gunmen inside were hunkered down, shoving their rifles out the windows to fire occasional blind bursts over the sills.

Bolan and Manning came on.

The Union Corse hardmen had unleashed over two thousand rounds into the garden. The trees were defoliated with bullet strikes. The lawn looked like it had been savaged by an army of gophers on crack. The alabaster Greek gods were cratered like the surface of the moon. Bolan fired a grenade through the first-floor kitchen window and the darkened room lit up with a flash of orange flame. Manning looped a grenade onto the third-floor balcony.

They mounted the patio. A man crouched by the barbecue yanked on his jammed rifle screaming, "Fuck you!"

Bolan shot him down and moved on. "Going in," he said.

The soldier stepped through the sliding patio door. The fragmentation grenades had done their lethal work in the confines of the living room. The dead and wounded lay strewed about. Bolan could see two more men lying in spreading pools of blood in the kitchen.

He could hear car engines revving.

Bolan and Manning loped to the front of the house. The front door was open, and three men had piled into an SUV while a fourth was limping and screaming after them as they pulled out of the garage. The engine howled in overdrive as the driver floored it in reverse.

Manning's launcher fired.

The windshield imploded and the rest of the windows in the truck exploded. The SUV rolled off the drive and began bucking and tumbling down the mountain trailing smoke.

The wounded gunman turned. He staggered as blood poured down his left leg. "I surrender! I fucking surrender!"

Bolan's submachine gun barked off a single shot. The man screamed as his right leg buckled beneath him.

"Stay down!"

The man lay on the driveway howling with bullets through both legs.

A Porsche and another SUV were still parked in the three-car garage. Bolan and Manning put a grenade into each vehicle, reducing them to ruin. The two warriors went back into the house.

People were screaming and yelling in French upstairs.

Bolan and Manning took turns covering each other as they swept from room to room, clearing the first floor and then moving up to the second. Bolan suspected Birkin had been on the master balcony for a panoramic view of the ambush.

Birkin had also treed himself.

Manning slid a fresh magazine into his weapon. "How do you want to play it?"

"By the numbers." Bolan loaded a flash-stun round into his grenade launcher. "Room by room." He launched the grenade up the stairs and squeezed his eyes shut and clenched his teeth at the blinding flash and the thunderclap.

Bolan charged up the stairs.

A gunman stood staggering on the landing, firing his rifle blindly. Bolan hammered him to the carpet with a 4-round burst of 10 mm flat-heads through the chest. Bolan kicked the first door he came to and found an empty bedroom.

Down the hall the door to the master bedroom flew open, and two men with automatic carbines came out firing from the hip.

Bolan and Manning dropped prone, both of them shooting. The two gunmen shuddered and toppled back into the bedroom. Someone inside slammed the door shut.

Bolan rose and reloaded. "You got another banger?"

"Yeah." Manning loaded a stun munition and they cleared the rest of the floor. All the rooms were empty save for the closed master bedroom.

Bolan nodded. "Do it."

They both dropped low again as the barrier-penetrating round smashed through the wooden door. Instantly long strings of rifle fire ripped outward in response. The door shook with the flash-bang's sonic clap and the rifles fell silent.

Bolan and Manning moved in for the kill.

The door flung open. The two warriors abruptly held their fire. Two women came screaming out of the room. They flew at Bolan and Manning in a weeping hysterical wave of lips and breasts and hips and hair. "Don't shoot! Please don't shoot!"

"Down!" Bolan ordered. "Get down!"

The women were half blinded and deafened by the stun grenade. They ran straight into Bolan and Manning shrieking.

Rifle fire erupted behind them.

One woman fell against Bolan. Her tan flesh shuddered and shook with bullet strike after bullet strike. Rifle rounds tore through the woman's body and struck Bolan's armor. He shoved his weapon past her, firing the submachine gun one-handed like a giant pistol. One of the riflemen fell, clutching his chest. Another leaped to take his place and two riflemen held their triggers down. They emptied their magazines, blasting the woman apart to get at Bolan. She collapsed, and Bolan took a full burst in the chest and lost his footing. He hit the floor and grimaced as the dead woman's knee smashed into his groin.

Manning was still shooting. The two riflemen in the doorway went down the hard way with bursts through the head. Manning's weapon ran dry and he dropped his submachine gun, slapping leather for his pistol.

The twin thunderclaps of a double-barrel boomed from inside the bedroom. Manning was blasted off of his feet as he took both barrels in the chest.

Another rifleman came through the door, slamming a fresh 100-round drum into his weapon. Bolan pushed his submachine gun up from under the dead woman and fired from the floor. His weapon rattled off two rounds and clacked open on empty.

The rifleman suddenly stood to attention. He reached a curious hand up to his face, probing his empty left eye socket and touching the black, bleeding hole over his left eyebrow. He sagged against the wall and slid to the floor.

Serge Birkin stepped out of the door. He was wearing a blue bathrobe and a cigarette dangled between his lips. He broke open the action of a sawed-off 10-gauge shotgun and plucked the spent shells from the smoking breech.

Manning lay on the floor next to the other dead girl, gasping like a fish.

Bolan himself could barely breathe from the hammering he'd taken and the weight of the woman on top of him. He released his spent submachine gun. The deadweight of the blonde covered his hips and made drawing his pistols impossible. Birkin's thick lips curled into a grin of cruelty. "You are fucked."

The Don of Quebec shoved in two fresh rounds of buckshot and snapped the shotgun shut.

Bolan rammed his hand between himself and the dead woman. Birkin's eyes widened at the motion and he yanked back the hammers of his shotgun. Bolan ripped the HAFLA hand-flame projector free of his belt. He thrust forth the 35 mm tube and pressed the button. The aluminum projectile blew out of the tube and struck Birkin in the sternum.

Birkin's shotgun roared and buckshot tore ragged holes in the wall behind Bolan's head.

The Executioner's vision whited out as Birkin became the center of an incendiary supernova. The Don was in the very center of the fifteen-foot fireball. Bolan flung his forearm across his eyes as searing heat washed over him in a wave. The hall was instantly filled with blinding, choking, burning coal-black smoke. Bolan struggled as the dead woman's hair ignited and flared on his chest. He heaved and rolled off the seared, burning body and crawled to Manning.

The big Canadian gagged and choked. Bolan grabbed him by his web belt and hauled him into a bathroom and slammed the door. The sprinkler system was on, but Bolan charged for the cavernous shower stall and threw the taps. He shoved Manning in as the eight brass showerheads all began blasting at once. Bolan thrust his partner's face beneath one of the icy streams to cool his flash-burned face.

Manning hacked and choked as Bolan stripped away their armor and web belt and hosed the smoldering particulate off them.

"You all right?"

Manning struggled for breath. "I feel like I got sat on by an elephant."

Bolan hosed off his holsters and drew his pistols. "Stay here. Rest a minute." He wet a hand towel in the sink and held it over his nose and mouth as he opened the door. Black smoke billowed into the bathroom. Bolan squinted and stepped into the hall. The smoke alarm was shrilling and the sprinkler system was showering everything. The water was preventing the fire from spreading but in the sphere of dispersion the Red Phosphorus compound would continue burning until it had consumed itself.

Serge Birkin lay on the floor. His limbs had folded and pulled into his blackened and shriveled corpse like a cricket. Blue flames that were still too bright to look at directly flickered over his form. Steam rose hissing from him as the fire suppression sprinklers rained on the molten metal still clinging to him.

Bolan hurdled Birkin's body. He stepped over the bodies of half a dozen dead hitters and went into the bedroom. He slammed the battered door behind him to stop the smoke and followed a trail of blood around a bed the size of a mountain range.

A thin black man lay with his head resting against the nightstand. He wore an immaculate black suit with a red silk shirt and a red silk pocket square. The spreading maroon stain on his right breast ruined his dapper appearance. His breath came in and out with a wheeze. Blood bubbled across his lips and in the hole in his shirt.

Mano Razanjato had a sucking chest wound.

Bolan lifted his head at the sound of sirens in the distance. "You look bad, Mano."

"Fuck…you."

"Who tipped you off that we were coming? Consolata?"

Mano spit blood.

Bolan lifted his boot over Mano's chest. "Who dropped the dime?"

"It was her…" Razanjato moaned.

"Where's the bacteria?"

The dying man's bloodshot eyes blinked. "What? What the hell—goddamn it! Shit!"

Bolan put some weight on the wound. "Where?"

"What?" The gangster screamed and gargled blood. "Where's what?"

Bolan leveled both of his pistols at the man's head. "Tell me and you live. Don't and you die."

The Desert Eagle and the Beretta clicked simultaneously as he threw off the safeties.

"The bacteria. You brewed it in Cape Breton. You had a containment failure, and it spread to Newfoundland. Where is it now?"

Mano Ranzajato was the right-hand man of the Don of Quebec. His boss had been burned to a crisp in front of him. He had a sucking chest wound and a foot on his sternum. He was blinking up into Bolan's guns in total incomprehension. "What?"

Bolan spun on his heel and went back down the hall. Birkin had burned out, as had the phosphorus clinging to the carpet and the walls and the ceiling. The hall was a blackened shell that stank of cooked bodies and burned metal. Bolan spoke into his com link. "Doc, we're extracting. Bring the car around."

"On my way. Is everything all right?"

"No." Bolan pushed open the bathroom door.

Manning was back on his feet and was rearmed and equipped. "What did you learn?"

"We got played."

"Played?" Manning shook his head. "What do you mean?"

"Birkin and his crew don't have the bacteria. They don't have anything to do with it." Bolan holstered his pistols "There's a new player we don't know about, and we just eliminated his competition."

15

Quebec

Lorenzo Renoir roared with laughter. "They clipped Birkin?"

"Him and his whole crew." Carlo Ettiene had to wipe tears from his eyes. "I swear, they lit up Serge with a fucking flamethrower or something. Fried his ass. The RCMP had to identify him through dental records. I'm telling you, he's a goddamn Tater-Tot."

"Carlo's right. I saw the coroner's photo." The Moor nearly spit beer out his nose he was laughing so hard. "Add cheese curds and gravy and he's fucking poutine."

"Cajun-style poutine," Sedin added.

The room reverberated with the mobsters' mirth. The incineration of Serge Birkin was an endless source of amusement. But it was not the only order of business.

"Any survivors?" The Boss asked.

Carlo struggled for breath. "A few. All severely wounded."

"What about Mano? He is dangerous, and the old men on both sides of the Atlantic respect him. He'll never be a Don, but he's a kingmaker, and he could cause us trouble."

"Razanjato's in intensive care with a bullet through his chest. They couldn't save his lung. The police found over two dozen automatic weapons on the premises, and two women were shot to death three meters from where they found Mano." Carlo poured himself two fingers of single malt. "Mano's going away for a long time."

Renoir leaned back in his chair and lit a celebratory cigar. By his calculations that left him the de facto boss of Quebec, if not the most powerful crime boss of all of French Canada.

It was good to be the king.

"Okay, enough sucking each other's dicks. We still lost Esau and the Spider."

"They were sick fucks." Carlo made a dismissive noise and flicked imaginary dust from the gleaming black leather of his shoes. "I will admit they were good earners, and approached their work with a certain joie de vivre, but any asshole can run porn and slaves. Killing people, and getting away with it, now that is hard." Carlo paused meaningfully. "And I miss The Jew already."

The Boss gazed around the table at his crew. "And this fuck, despite the favor he did for us this morning, is still alive and gunning for us."

The Moor cracked himself another beer. "His ass is already designated dead."

The Boss raised an eyebrow. "Your plan is in motion, then?"

"The only question is whether you want him to die smiling—" The Moor shrugged back his long black hair "—or if you want him delivered unto us."

Carlo frowned. "Rumor is he had someone helping him at Birkin's."

The Boss sneered. "That doctor? I got something in mind for his ass."

"No, some new fucking hardcase. From what I could find out it's like our boy cloned himself."

Renoir's massive brow knitted as he sipped Pernod. "Kara says the bacteria will be ready by the end of the week. I want this American shithead dead before then. I want his little friend dead, and I want that fucking doctor dead."

"The American we have a line on." The Moor chased his beer with a shot of whiskey. "His mystery clone, he's an unknown, but we get the American, we'll get his buddy, and the American is dead within forty-eight hours, guaranteed."

The Boss wasn't satisfied. "What about the goddamn doctor?"

Carlo lit himself a cigarette. "Ferentinos? He's part of the Canadian Government's investigation. He's gotta surface sooner or later. When he does, we take him."

"Yeah, well, we shot the doctor, and we shot this fucking commando, and they still won't die." The Boss smiled suddenly. "Speaking of which, I got what you asked for, Carlo."

Renoir was a large man, but he grunted with effort as he lifted an oversized plastic rifle case from the floor and dumped it on the table. He shoved the case toward Ettiene. "That what you wanted?"

Ettiene flipped the latches. He grinned as he lifted the lid and examined the case's contents. The case contained a PGM Hecate II 12.7 mm sniper rifle. The massive, modular rifle fired the U.S. .50-caliber heavy machine gun round. Three boxes of ammunition were packed in the case. Carlo took out a gleaming metal cartridge. The steel-jacketed bullet weighed six and a half times as much as the 9 mm rounds in his pistol, and flew just shy of three thousand feet per second. It was a round that would pierce a light-armored vehicle.

"Yeah." He placed the round back in the case and closed it. "It's exactly what I wanted."

"Good. Then we all know what to do."

The celebration was over. It was time to get back to work.

There was a knock on the door and Laurent Courvier leaned into the conference room grinning. "Boss, you have a visitor."

Renoir stared deeply into his tumbler. "I'm busy."

Laurent was grinning from ear to ear. "I really think you want to take this one."

Renoir was in a benevolent mood. "Fine, what the fuck. Send him in."

The door opened and conversation fell silent. It was the kind of effect Consolata Malatesta had when she entered a room. The black dress she wore hugged her every curve. A phalanx of her bodyguards stood in the reception area behind her. She ran her gray eyes around the room, stopping momentarily on Gaultier "The Moor" Salamanca and then falling upon Renoir. "We have to talk," was all she said.

"Sure." The Boss opened his hand graciously and then waved it in a circle to his crew. "Boys, give me a few minutes."

The crew filed out, their eyes lingering on the woman's flesh.

"Have a seat." The Boss pushed a box across the table. "Cigarette?"

She lifted her perfectly sculpted chin slightly and sneered at his offer.

"You know what I want," she said.

"You want his head." Renoir nodded. "We both do."

"I want more than his head." The gray eyes went steely. "I want a percentage."

Renoir snorted. "A percentage of what?"

"Of what you're up to." Malatesta poured herself a whiskey.

"I don't know what you're talking about."

"The American came. He violated my house and assaulted my father."

"Yeah, I heard about that." Renoir's eyes narrowed as he swirled the liquid in his glass. "So, what did you two talk about?"

"He wanted the Mountie, of course, and the men who had taken her."

"Yeah, well, he fucking got them." Renoir's bloated face went ugly. "And fuck you very much for giving up my men."

"He had an AK-47 to my father's head. I had to tell him something." The woman smiled in mock empathy. "However, what I didn't tell him was that I suspected The Moor had flipped to your crew. He still thinks Buriz, the Spider and Salamanca all worked for Birkin. Now Birkin, Buriz and the Spider are all dead. Mano is in hospital and the American has lost the cooperation of the RCMP."

"Yeah, well, I'll admit that it's a fortuitous chain of events, but it wasn't like you masterminded it. You knew enough to keep your mouth shut and things fell out the way they did."

"Yes, but I am the one who called Serge. I told him the man who had hit my family and killed Buriz and the Spider would be coming for him within forty-eight hours. That gave him time to gather his soldiers."

"Yeah, and Birkin got himself and his whole crew toasted."

The office was air-conditioned, but Malatesta took an ice cube from her drink and ran it casually across her collarbones. Renoir watched her clavicles gleam. She continued speaking. "And now you are unofficially the head of the Union Corse in Canada. There are old men who will resist, but you will end up on top. You are young and hungry, and many others who are hungry will flock to you." She shrugged elegantly. "But if Birkin's men had succeeded in killing the American, then I would still have solved a problem for you. Either way, you won."

"So I owe you." Renoir finished his drink and grinned. "I still don't know what fucking percentage you're talking about."

"The American came to my house for the Mountie. My sources tell me the Mountie bitch came from Newfoundland, and was working on the flesh-eating outbreak they were having on the Rock. The investigation led them here. The Mountie was being made an example of. That meant movies. That meant Buriz and the Spider. They work for The Moor, and like I said, I had figured out some time ago that Salamanca had flipped to you. You're making a weapon, and you're going to sell it. I want a piece of the action."

Renoir's eyes were slits. "Or you'll give me up?"

"I didn't say that."

Renoir's scarred hands closed into fists. "I can whack you right now."

"I have eight men outside, all heavy. You want a war, we can finish each other off right here and some pissant nickel and dimers will rise up in our place rather than eating our table scraps. You are now the top man in the Union Corse in Canada in all but name. I am now ruling the Italians in this province as regent for my father. What I'm saying is that an alliance would be advantageous for both of us. The American is still loose. The RCMP is in full investigation mode. You may have need of my resources." She drooped her heavy lashes. "And you owe me."

Renoir's face was stony. "I'll give you five percent."

"I want fifteen.'

"Yeah?" Renoir leaned back in his chair and examined the smoke curling out of his cigar. "What about what I want?"

"Ah." The woman rose from the chair. She slowly shrugged her dress from her shoulders and Renoir watched in unblinking awe as her gravity defying flesh spilled forth. She stared into Renoir's eyes like a snake hypnotizing its prey as she slowly hiked her dress up around her hips. The Don's daughter was not wearing any underwear. She leaned over the table until her palms and elbows rested on it. Consolata Malatesta raised a coal black eyebrow in challenge.

"I know what you want."

Lorenzo Renoir rose from his chair. He drew his revolver and unzipped his fly.

It was good to be the king.

Montreal

INSPECTOR FAITH GELINAS looked like a piece of art as she walked through the door. Her golden brown hair, golden brown skin and golden brown eyes almost matched. She wasn't in uniform and she looked good in jeans. She was the only woman in Fat Fingers. The woman took a seat at the table and looked around the gay bar with curious amusement. "Nice place."

"Yeah, well." Bolan shrugged and poured her a glass of beer from his pitcher. "No one's looking for a guy like me here."

The inspector's generous lips quirked.

"How's Dani?" Bolan asked.

"Better. A lot better. They should be releasing her today."

Bolan looked at the manila folder in Gelinas's hand. "You have something for me?"

"Maybe." She opened the file and held up a photo. 'Recognize him?"

Bolan took in the long black hair and flat, sharklike eyes. "Gaultier Salamanca. The Moor."

"That's right. Esau Buriz was a big earner for The Moor, and the Spider was Esau's associate."

"I know, and before I lost the love of the RCMP The Moor had gone missing."

"Well, there's a rumor that he's more than missing. Rumor is he may have flipped."

"To the Feds?" Bolan asked.

"No, to a different crew." Gelinas held up another photo. "You know this guy?"

Bolan had looked at dozens of RCMP, FBI and Interpol files on Canadian criminals in the past seventy-two hours, and this was a face he'd seen. "Lorenzo Renoir. He's on my list, but he isn't near the top."

"He's off a lot of people's radar. Renoir's rumored to have a lot of people earning for him, but he does his business a lot more professionally than a lot of the old mobsters. He works through cutouts. No one's been able to get an undercover agent anywhere near him, and a great deal of his illegal activities seem to happen offshore. He's heavily connected across the Atlantic. A lot of police agencies have him pegged as an intermediary between the North American and European Union Corse Families, but for some time there has been talk that he's been making moves, and getting involved with things outside the normal organized crime activities. Nothing anyone could put their finger on."

"Like supplying North African extremists with biological weapons."

"We can't tie the Skir Dhu distillery or the fire to him, and no evidence of the bacteria was found in the ruins."

"Both Buriz and Salamanca spent a lot of time in Algeria and Tunisia."

"The RCMP has almost no information on their activities there, other than allegations of slave trading and gunrunning. What little information we had came from Interpol. Frankly I was hoping you could shed some light on it."

"I have people working on it. As soon as I have something, I'll pass it along to you. You have anything else?"

The RCMP inspector frowned. "I have this." She pushed a piece of paper across the table. An address was written on it.

Bolan's instincts spoke. "The Moor."

"Wow, I'm impressed." The inspector stared into her beer. "You know The Moor is not officially wanted for anything. Anything you do…" The inspector's voice trailed away.

Bolan knew all too well. "Where's Waskaganish?"

"That's northern Quebec, on Rupert Bay. Salamanca owns a hunting-fishing lodge up there." Gelinas frowned. "And what are you smiling about?"

"Nothing." Bolan was thinking about Gary Manning. The big Canadian hunter was tailor-made for a fire mission above the 52nd parallel.

They were going to need a plane.

The inspector's eyes narrowed. "You know, I think Dani made a big mistake."

"What's that?"

"She should have slept with you."

Bolan smiled easily. "Let's hope she learns from her mistakes."

The inspector's enormous golden-brown eyes were staring into Bolan's very steadily. He was tempted to enjoy the inspector's unspoken offer, but he had plans to arrange and unfinished business with The Moor.

16

Northern Quebec

"What do you think?" Manning asked.

Bolan scanned the 2.5 power optical sight of his sound suppressed Steyr Scout rifle across the landscape. "It's too quiet."

"I hate it when you say that."

Bolan shrugged.

The landscape was nothing short of majestic. The low, arid mountains were studded by stands of equally low and thin conifers. As they had flown in, the land beneath them had unrolled in a patchwork of silver rivers and blue lakes. It was the 52nd Parallel, the no-man's land between the endless Canadian arboreal forest and the vast open tundra. It was harsh, unforgiving land, and in the brief blossoming moments of summer it was beautiful beyond words.

The hunting lodge had been built to take maximum advantage of the surroundings. It was a rambling two-story structure that hugged the hillside with a stable and a barn. The lodge was surrounded by trees but overlooked a series of finger lakes and the open land that rolled downward toward Rupert Bay.

Bolan had no doubt that hunters had paused on that exact spot for thousands of years to survey the territory ahead.

He scanned The Moor's hunting lodge again. A single Land Rover was parked out in the drive. One of the three chimneys had smoke curling up out of it.

"Jack, give me a flyby."

Jack Grimaldi came back across the com link. "Roger that, Sarge. ETA five minutes." Stony Man Farm's ace pilot had picked them up in Montreal, and they had rented the DHC-2 Beaver floatplane in Waskaganish. Bolan and Manning had stepped out onto the pontoons at four thousand feet and parachuted into the interior. They had spent the afternoon humping their way through miles of rolling forestland in full battle gear to approach the lodge at dusk.

The plan was simple. Approach the lodge, hit silently, snatch The Moor and extract to the nearest lake where Grimaldi would be waiting in the float plane. Everything was going according to plan.

Bolan didn't like it at all.

The low drone of the Beaver's radial engine became audible as the plane skimmed over the trees. The blue-and-yellow plane buzzed overhead and off toward the bay as a dozen flights did every day ferrying hunters and fishermen out into the interior and then home again to the coastal towns.

The radio crackled in Bolan's earpiece. "Sarge, I have no movement. You want me to go over again?"

"Negative. Orbit at distance, we'll call for extraction."

Bolan and Manning spread apart and moved through

the trees toward their target. Manning suddenly stopped and held up his fist. The big Canadian crouched and motioned Bolan over. The soldier dropped to his heels beside him. Manning had out his Cold Steel Outdoorsman knife and was clearing away some pine needles with the tip of its blade. In the uncertain light Bolan could discern a thin, taut piece of monofilament wire stretched between the trees three inches off the ground. Even in broad daylight a moving man would have been likely to step right through it. It was only detectable at the moment because of a few dry pine needles that had fallen and were hung up on it.

Bolan followed the wire to where it was wrapped around a tree. Behind the trunk was a French Lacroix trip flare. Anyone breaking the wire would set off the blank signal cartridge that would make a sound louder than a gunshot and the flare would light up the area with about 4,500 candlepower's worth of light for six minutes.

Manning smiled at the device. "Not your typical mob burglar alarm."

"A lot more typical of a French Foreign Legion parachute commando securing his perimeter." Bolan agreed. "Question is, is it old or new?"

Manning went to the tree and stared at the launcher long and hard. He very gently probed the tip of his knife around the screws holding the trip flare against the tree and then examined his blade. "The sap is fairly fresh. Gelled rather than crystallized. I'm saying this perimeter was emplaced twenty-four hours ago, tops." He looked at the seemingly quiet lodge. "Whoever's in there has gone to a high state of alert."

Bolan stared at the trip flare. The entire perimeter would be wired. There was only one vehicle outside. There was smoke coming from the chimney. Bolan's instincts spoke to him. Gaultier "The Moor" Salamanca might have owned the deed to the place, but Bolan had no doubt in his mind.

They were deep in Carlo Ettiene country.

"We've been set up." Manning sheathed his blade with a sigh. "Again."

Bolan clicked open his phone and pressed a preset number.

Antonetti picked up the first ring. "Jesus, Cooper, where the hell have you been?"

"Tell me all you know about RCMP Inspector Faith Gelinas."

"Who?"

"I'll get back to you." Bolan clicked the phone shut.

"The inspector screwed us." Manning stated the obvious."

Bolan clicked his com link. "Jack, we need extraction now, primary site. We may be coming in hot."

"Affirmative, Sarge inbound. Three minutes."

"You know?" Manning continued peering at the French perimeter alarm. "There's an extra bit of wire here going up the trunk, almost like an antenna— Jesus!"

The blank cartridge cracked like a rifle shot. Manning threw himself to one side and rolled to his feet as the igniting flare sent up a geyser of blinding white fire six feet in the air.

Someone had detected their presence and radio detonated the flare.

Engines snarled into life. The doors to the garage, the barn and the stable flew open. ATVs came roaring out like an army of all-terrain Hell's Angels. Bolan snapped his Steyr up to his shoulder and flicked off the safety.

The range was three hundred yards. Bolan put his crosshairs on the lead rider and fired. The sound suppressed rifle softly recoiled against his shoulder. The rider toppled back across the rear of his ATV as if an invisible linebacker had clotheslined him. Bolan flicked his bolt and swung his sights onto his next target. Gary Manning's rifle coughed a few feet away and another rider fell forward over his handlebars and succeeded in running himself over as he fell beneath his own wheels.

Bolan's left eye was still open and taking in his surroundings as he shot. In the slanting rays of the setting sun he saw the small orange circle appear in the darkened upstairs window of the loft. It was sunlight reflecting on glass.

Someone had optics on them.

Bolan threw his shoulder into Manning. "Down!"

Orange flame belched out of the loft like a cannon firing.

Bolan flew backward until a tree brutally interrupted his flight path. His body slapped against the tree and then he toppled facefirst into the forest mulch.

"Mack!" Manning was shouting. "Mack!"

Bolan tried to do a push-up and collapsed back into the pine needles.

Hands seized Bolan's web belt and he was dragged behind the cover of the tree. "You all right?"

Bolan blinked. He couldn't draw breath. Manning was

ripping at the tabs of his body armor. Bolan's half-focused eyes saw his rifle on the ground a few feet away. The fore stock was smashed, and the cold-forged, fluted steel barrel was bent at a right angle.

"That's a .50-caliber!" Manning pulled a deformed, three-inch-long bullet out of Bolan's vest and checked the integrity of his armor. "Your trauma plate's shattered. You're not." He grabbed Bolan's spare Steyr magazines.

Bolan felt shattered. His rifle and armor had prevented the bullet from ripping through him, but his body had still been forced to absorb and distribute the five tons of kinetic energy. The giant rifle in the loft roared again. Bolan and Manning flinched as a fist-sized hole exploded from the tree trunk inches above their head.

Their cover was no cover at all.

Manning pulled Bolan's Beretta and Desert Eagle pistols from their holsters and shoved them into the Executioner's hands. "Let's go!" He hauled Bolan up by his armor and the two warriors broke into a stumbling run.

The ATVs were closing.

"Can you shoot?" Manning asked.

Bolan blinked and shook his head, but he couldn't clear it. "I see two of everything."

"Shoot both," Manning suggested.

Bolan flicked off the pistols' safeties. The snarls of the ATV engines were behind them and now ahead on their left. Behind them the giant rifle thundered and a sapling was blasted in two a foot to Manning's right. "They're trying to herd us into the open ground!"

Bolan thumbed his throat mike. "Jack, we're heading back toward the lodge.

"Affirmative, Sarge."

Bolan turned on his pursuers, his pistols spitting fire and rolling with recoil in his hands. The lead ATV popped a wheelie and cracked its axles against a tree as its driver took rounds from both of Bolan's weapons. Manning was flicking his bolt and firing as fast as he could acquire targets. The two men headed for the lodge, through the jaws of the trap and right down its throat.

The .50-caliber rifle in the loft boomed again, throwing up an explosion of dirt and pine needles where Bolan had just been. Manning worked two quick rounds through the loft window and dodged. They charged forward, weaving through the trees. They closed to fifty yards. The immense antimaterial rifle perched upstairs boomed, but it was too big and heavy to traverse against moving targets.

The flamethrower was not.

"Jesus!" Manning threw himself in the mud as a fifty-yard-long sheet of fire spewed through tree line. "I'm starting to hate this Carlo guy!"

Bolan hugged a fold in the ground as the heat wave rolled over and pine needles above his head blackened. He thumbed his mike. "You see that, Jack?"

"I saw it, Sarge. Be advised you have men dismounting ATVs behind you in squad strength and fanning out toward your position. Half a dozen are still mounted and hanging back as a mobile reserve."

The trap had slammed shut.

Bolan glanced at Manning. Trees burned like torches before them. The giant sniper rifle would be scanning the devastation, waiting for them to pop up. The infantry would drive them forward into the light support weapons facing them. There was only one thing to do.

"We have to take the lodge," Bolan said.

"Okay." Manning rolled his eyes. "You run down the .50. I'll charge the flamethrower."

"Deal." Bolan nodded.

"Uh…" Manning could never be quite sure when Bolan was joking.

Bolan thumbed his mike. "Jack, we need air support, ASAP."

Grimaldi paused as he considered his air support options. "Options are limited, Sarge." The pilot clearly wasn't pleased. "Inbound."

Manning's rifle whispered, and a man behind them slumped against a tree. A half-dozen automatic rifles ripped back at them in response. Bolan watched the muzzle-flashes in the gloom and picked off two men with his pistols. The Desert Eagle clacked open and he was out of spare magazines. Heat billowed and more trees flared up in liquid fire as the man with the flamethrower sought them.

Bolan clicked the folding fore grip of the Beretta 93-R and took the machine pistol in both hands. "Anytime, Jack."

"Setting autopilot. You better give me a diversion or they're going to be skeet shooting on my happy ass."

"On your go," Bolan confirmed.

"I'm sorry, baby. You're a beautiful girl, and you done good. You know I love you," Jack Grimaldi said to his plane.

Bolan could hear the deep drone of the radial engine.

He glanced up. The Beaver was at about eight hundred feet. The angle of descent was steep to say the least.

"Jack."

"Just a sec—"

"Get out of there, Jack."

The big .50-caliber rifle in the loft fired again, and the tracer streaked through the sky and slammed into the Beaver's fuselage.

Grimaldi was getting dangerously underneath the minimum altitude for a base jump.

"I need that diversion...." The pilot was checking his angle and speed a final time. 'Now! See ya!"

Bolan began firing off bursts from his machine pistol. Manning's rifle coughed in rapid fire. The gunmen in the trees responded. The rifle in the lodge boomed as fast as the sniper could work his bolt, and every shot shook the oncoming plane. Seven hundred feet up a tiny figure clambered out onto the pilot-side pontoon and stepped into space.

Bolan slammed in his last magazine and fired burst after burst. He glanced upward and saw Grimaldi fling his drogue chute. The pilot plummeted for another moment, and then his main shoot deployed. Bolan dropped his spent machine pistol. "Gary! I'm out!"

Manning drew his Browning Hi-Power and tossed it to Bolan.

The Beaver roared overhead. Her massive engine was making unnatural clanking noises as the big .50 chopped into it. The plane continued, her angle of descent and speed set by the autopilot. The big rifle suddenly stopped firing. The flamethrower man raised his aim and the

Beaver was sheathed in flame. The 5,000-pound plane slammed into the hunting lodge at 150 miles per hour.

Bolan rose from cover and charged.

Half of the lodge was a smoking ruin. The other half was on fire. Pieces of it were still raining to the ground. The flamethrower man had been taking cover behind the well but had run out and thrown himself to the drive just before the plane hit. He was up on one knee. He spun his projector around as Manning came out of the burning trees. His 12,000-volt igniter arced blue beneath his muzzle as he squeezed the first of his double triggers in preparation to burn down Manning.

The Hi-Power barked in Bolan's hand. Two of the 9 mm hollowpoint rounds hit the man in the side. Two more struck the flamethrower's fuel tank and a fifth hit the pressurization cylinder. The high-pressure cylinder ruptured.

The flamethrower man ignited into a screaming, expanding ball of jellied jet fuel.

The lodge was burning out of control. The drive was a series of burning pools of fuel. The surrounding forest was an arc of choking black smoke and fire reaching for the skies.

Manning said, "I'll go around back."

The front door was still vaguely attached to its door frame. Bolan kicked it in and entered the burning building. A man with an M-16 rifle was screaming into a cell phone.

Bolan blasted him with a double-tap to the chest and moved on. There were more targets within. The Executioner advanced towards the sound of shouting near the back. Gunfire erupted. The shouts turned to screams as the assassins found themselves in Manning's sights.

Two panicked men with pistols came running and snapped around in surprise as they saw the Executioner. They raised their weapons too late as he hammered them with the Hi-Power.

A bullet smashed into a bookcase beside Bolan's head. Down the hall he could see a figure in the smoke on the other side of the kitchen. Bolan went flat against the wall and touched off two rounds. He crouched as the figure fired back. The soldier moved forward firing again. He saw the muzzle-flash of the enemy gun and fired twice more.

Bolan's pistol clacked open on empty.

Beyond the kitchen he heard a revolver click twice as the hammer dropped on a spent cylinder.

Carlo Ettiene staggered out of the smoke and carnage into the kitchen. The cabinets had been flung open by the plane's impact and broken appliances and tableware lay everywhere. Ettiene's suit hung in burned shreds around his body. His right eyebrow hung from his face in a bloody flap. He held a claw hammer loosely in his right hand. A bent cigarette hung unlit from his lip. The Frenchman leaned into the smoldering kitchen door frame and stuck his cigarette against the glowing wood, drawing until it lit. He inhaled deeply and smiled in satisfaction as he blew the smoke at the already shrieking smoke alarm.

"Kamikaze, huh?" Ettiene shrugged in lazy admiration and hefted his hammer toward Bolan. "Fuck you."

Bolan dropped his spent pistol. He drew his LaGana

titanium blade tactical tomahawk with his right hand.
His Recon Tanto knife filled his left in an ice-pick grip
as he took his fighting stance.

Ettiene smiled happily. The Frenchman reached into
a kitchen drawer and came out holding a massive knife
of curved steel. Ettiene raised his remaining eyebrow as
he brandished the blade.

Bolan kept his eyes on the hammer. Ettiene was absently rolling it back and forth in his hand, first presenting the claw and then the hammer peen.

Ettiene lunged, hammer first, moving with the grace
and speed of a trained fencing master. He snapped his
wrist, blurring the peen toward Bolan's temple. The Executioner blocked with his tomahawk. The knife blades
rang as Bolan deflected the saber stroke aimed at his
neck. Carlo spun his hammer in his grip, suddenly hooking Bolan's tomahawk haft with the claw. They wrestled,
locked together almost nose to nose, hammer to hatchet
and blade to blade, jockeying for the kill shot.

Ettiene spit his burning cigarette into Bolan's face.

The soldier shut his eyes against the sparks and turned
his hip, instinctively blocking the knee that Ettiene shot
up at his groin. Bolan rammed his head forward. His
forehead was already a massive bone bruise from the
head butt he had received from Esau Buriz less than forty-eight hours ago. Bolan saw stars and nausea buckled his
knees as his brow slammed into Ettiene's cheekbone.
The Frenchman staggered as his face fractured. Bolan
opened his eyes, staying focused through the blinking
lights before his eyes and attacked. Ettiene raised his
weapons defensively before his face. He folded as Bolan

sank the tomahawk into his stomach, then went rigid as his adversary stabbed his knife into his right kidney.

Bolan knelt below the smoke and took a deep breath. The kitchen was beginning to burn in earnest. "Gary, what have you got?"

"I got four hostiles down at the back door. Two more ran back."

"They're accounted for."

"What about Carlo?"

"Accounted for."

"Good. I hated that guy."

Bolan went into the front of the house and picked up a fallen rifle. "Jack, what is your situation?"

"I'm in a tree."

"Enemy disposition?"

"After the plane hit the lodge most of them got back on their ATVs and headed west. Two came creeping your way, but I handled them."

"We'll come for you."

Bolan went to the kitchen. He slung his rifle and dragged Carlo Ettiene by his heels. Manning was already out front hot-wiring the Land Rover. The front end was scorched, but the engine turned over under Manning's manipulations. Bolan threw Ettiene's body in the back. They piled in and drove out through the spreading forest fire.

Grimaldi's voice came across the wire. "I see you. I'm twenty yards to your left."

Manning pulled the vehicle off the road. Night was falling and everything was lit orange by the fires.

"You're below me."

Bolan got out and looked up. Grimaldi hung from a tree by his harness. In one hand he held his submachine gun. His other arm was hanging at a bad angle. His face was a mass of smeared blood and pine sap.

"You all right?" Bolan asked.

Grimaldi shrugged in his straps. "Just hanging out."

Bolan nodded wearily. "Let's get out of here.

17

Montreal

"Is that her?"

Bolan stared at the picture on his laptop screen.

The RCMP sketch artist appeared on his laptop.

"That's her," he said.

The commissioner stared at the sketch and compared it to a photo attached to a thick file. "That's a match." He turned the file around for the web camera. "You agree?"

Bolan stared into the face of the woman who had tried to seduce him and had set him up for a .50-caliber funeral. "That's her. I'm assuming she isn't an inspector of the RCMP."

"No, she certainly isn't."

"Who is she?" Bolan asked.

"Her name is Faye Ganzaga. She's Basque with French citizenship. She was a starlet in the French porn industry and into some very rough trade. She also associated with known members of Basque Separatist terror cells. She was arrested for assaulting an undercover detective. France got too hot for her and she moved to Spain for a while. Her activities there are unknown. She turned up in North Africa in 2002 where—"

"Where she met Salamanca."

"She's been Gaultier Salamanca's girlfriend for several years. She's wanted in Tunisia and Algeria for questioning in connection with a trio of murders. The three deceased were known to be involved in the North African slave trade, and rumored to have been competitors of The Moor."

Bolan checked at the other window on his screen. "Bear, what have you got on Carlo?"

"The good news is the French are playing ball with us. We sent Action Direct copies of fingerprints you took. They match French police files for Chavel MalCroix. If there's one thing the French Foreign Legion hates, it's deserters. Their records match. Chavel MalCroix and Carlo Ettiene are the same man."

"And unfortunately," in the commissioner broke, "you killed him before he could be detained and questioned."

Bolan shrugged. "He didn't give me much choice."

The commissioner stared at Bolan long and hard. "If I knew where you were, I would have you arrested."

"I know."

Manning was busy across the table on a laptop of his own. He was out of sight of the web cams carrying the conversation. He spun his computer silently and pointed. Akira Tokaido was on the screen.

The young hacker was grinning like he had won the lottery.

Bolan turned to his own screen. "Commissioner, I appreciate your candor, and while I am currently unwilling to surrender to the Canadian authorities I will continue to share information as I get it."

"So far what you've shared has been dead bodies, but—"

"Cooper, out."

Bolan punched keys, closing the commissioner's screen and opening Akira's. "Tell me it's Christmas."

"I got a little something for you." Tokaido punched a key and a website appeared on Bolan's screen. "I got you Le Distillerie du Cheval Sauvage."

Manning grinned. "Check out the accent on the kid."

Bolan read the promotional information on the website. The Wild Horse Distillery was a small operation, a start-up and less than a year old. It was in Quebec.

Bolan nodded. "What else have you got on them?"

"They're part of a larger, French-owned consortium."

"And?"

"There were a lot of cutouts, and it took a lot of hacking, but controlling interest of the Wild Horse distillery appears to be held by a circle of investors in—"

"Corsica," Bolan guessed.

"That's right. All import-export men."

"Import-export" was slang for smuggling in every country on Earth, and the Corsicans had been smugglers and pirates since the days of wooden ships.

"What else have you got on them?"

"Nothing." Tokaido smiled and shrugged. "Wild Horse appears to be a completely legit operation. They pay their taxes, their distilling licenses are all in order, they started producing limited runs of whiskey a year ago and Canucks in selected cities have been happily gargling with it ever since. They're turning a profit, and according to their prospectus they intend to open a sister distillery on the West Coast next year. They're above board."

"Any connection with the distillery in Cape Breton?"

"We haven't found one yet, but we're looking."

Bolan leaned back in his chair. "You guys want to hit a distillery?"

His team looked back at him. Jack Grimaldi had eaten a pine tree at twenty miles per hour and his face was lumped with abrasions and contusions. He'd also hyperextended his left elbow and broken his right thumb. Manning looked better, save that the flamethrower had gotten close enough to sear off his eyebrows and leave him looking like he'd gotten a bad sunburn.

Bolan ached with every breath.

Grimaldi grinned. "I need a drink."

Quebec

"YOU SHOULD HAVE GIVEN them to me." The six-inch switchblade clacked open and clicked closed as Faye Ganzaga manically pressed the twin chrome skulls of its action. "The American and the Mountie slut. I could have taken them both out at the same time. It would have been…fun." Ugliness moved behind Ganzaga's eyes.

Gaultier Salamanca knew his woman's moods all too well. "You can have the Professor. We're done with him."

"Professor Jov? I've seen the way he looks at me." She scowled. "That shriveled old Russian—"

"And his wife." The Moor smiled. Renoir was smiling as well. "We're done with her, too."

"Carlo's dead," Big Damage said. "And you're all talking about snuffing Russians."

The Moor frowned. "But the American is out of leads."

"He knows me, he knows you and now he knows Faye." Sedin looked at Renoir. "And at this point you gotta be high on his list there, Chief. If we show our faces, he's gonna blow them off. Fact is, we're hiding from him." Sedin shrugged and stretched the Hawthorns. "I don't like hiding."

"Neither do I," Renoir said. "But we are just about to make the biggest score of our lives, and I don't want any fuck-ups. Moor, take Lawrence and his crew, do the facility, just like last time. No traces, no loose ends."

"I'm on it." Salamanca began pushing buttons on his cell phone. "I'll have everything staged for final delivery."

"Good." Renoir smiled at Ganzaga. "Like The Moor said, we're finished with the Russians. Why don't you tie up that one for me?"

Her smile went feral as she closed her switchblade.

"What about the American? What about his goddamn little buddy?" Sedin scowled. "And unless the pilot of that plane was some Jap who still doesn't know the war is over, they got some new asshole willing to fling planes into ground targets. That makes three."

"Three is all they got. They've broken every fucking police procedure in Canada. They can't show their faces, just like us, except that we don't need to. We just take care of business, and they have to come to us." Renoir finished his Scotch. "And there's only one place possible where that might happen."

18

"Don't tell me." Gary Manning lay in the grass, scanning the distillery through his night optics. "It's too quiet."

Bolan crouched in the trees holding a sound suppressed Parker-Hale Individual Defensive Weapon like an oversized pistol in each hand. "You tell me."

"I don't know." Manning's IDW had been converted to light support weapon mode with a shoulder stock, a sound suppressed fourteen-inch barrel, bipod and a sniper scope. He ran his optics around the perimeter again and grinned out of the black greasepaint covering his face. "It's too quiet."

Jack leaned against a tree and watched the river roll by. His left arm was in a sling. His MAC-10 hung casually from his right hand. "I say we bust in and see what's really being brewed here."

"You see any security?" Bolan asked.

"No infrared lasers visible on any frequency." Manning adjusted the gain on his optics. "I don't see any trip wires. No guards in sight. No cars in the parking lot. What you got, visible, is a chain-link fence with a padlock. No telling what may be hooked up to that. Passive motion sensors, closed circuit alarms, hidden cameras, magnetometers, ten thousand volts..." Manning shrugged into the buttstock of his weapon. "Who knows? But we know Carlo was serious about security."

Bolan flicked off the safeties to his weapons and headed out of the trees.

Grimaldi grinned. "He's going rolling thunder on us." The pilot hurried forward, staying on Bolan's six. Manning stayed in the trees and covered them.

The Executioner's weapons hissed and cycled in his hands as he shot off the fence's padlock. He put his boot into the gate and it swung back on its hinges. Manning moved into a better covering position as the Executioner descended upon the distillery. The two IDWs in his hands were silent save for the clicking as their actions cycled. The heavy, subsonic 9 mm hollowpoint rounds made noises like whips cracking as they hammered the glass of the distillery public entrance. The glass spiderwebbed and collapsed as it was shot to shards.

Bolan slid fresh 30-round magazines into his weapons. Shattered glass crunched beneath his feet as he entered the lobby. Grimaldi went in behind him. The lobby was empty. Bolan spotted the security camera and put a burst through it.

"Well, if we haven't set off the silent alarm yet..." the pilot opined.

The soldier kicked open the lobby door and sidestepped.

Half a dozen shotguns roared. Bolan and Grimaldi pressed themselves on either side of the doorjamb as buckshot tore at the door frame.

"Gary." Bolan pulled the pin on a French SAE 210 hand grenade. "I need you."

"Affirmative, Striker."

Buckshot plucked at Bolan's sleeve as he tossed the grenade around the door frame. The walls of the lobby shook and orange light strobed as the grenade detonated. The overpressure washed out of the hallway in a hot wave. Bolan came around the door firing. There were three men in the hall. One lay unmoving and another screamed as he clutched the bloody socket where his arm had been torn from his shoulder. The third waved a shotgun dazedly as he bled from his eyes, nose and ears.

Bolan put him down with a burst from both of his weapons.

Grimaldi looked down the smoking hallway and the metal door leading to the distilling floor. "You know they're waiting for us."

"I know." Bolan turned as Manning came up behind them fitting a rifle grenade to the launching rings of his light support weapon. He smiled.

The steel door sagged, partially melted on its remaining hinge. Manning's round was designed to destroy a barrier but do little physical damage behind it.

Bolan knelt to avoid return fire. "Hit 'em again."

Manning clicked a flash-bang onto his weapon. Bolan and his team shut their eyes as a grenade sailed through the door and detonated in the middle of the distillery floor. Bolan was up as the thunderclap rattled the walls. He put his boot to the slagged door and stepped into the whirling flurry of sparking secondary effect.

A pair of stunned men stood waving their pistols. Bolan cut them down and moved deeper into the distillery. Four giant stills, twelve feet tall and sixteen feet around, dominated the room. Metal ladders led up each still, and a crucifix of catwalks connected them from above. Beyond the stills a small office looked down on the distillery floor. Men in the office smashed out the windows with their rifle butts.

Bolan's weapons bucked in his hands, and a man screamed and fell from the window to the concrete floor thirty feet below. The soldier ducked behind one of the huge stills as rifle fire answered back. A man popped out from behind the far still.

Bolan recognized him from the RCMP files he'd studied. The man's name was Laurent Courvier. He was Renoir's right-hand man. Bolan's weapons rattled off bursts.

The killer took the hits. A bright red dot swung along the still next to Bolan, seeking his face. The Executioner jerked aside as Courvier's shotgun thudded. Bolan flinched as orange fire lit up three feet from his head. Whiskey hit him in a spray from the ragged, fist-sized hole that had appeared in the steel cylinder. Bolan backed up as the shotgun fired twice more. The orange fire blossomed and the acrid stench of high explosive mixed with the eye-burning reek of alcohol.

"High explosive slugs." Manning spoke in Bolan's earpiece. "And this place probably has around sixty thousand gallons of alcohol in it."

Shotguns were firing all along the back of the distillery. The ruby dots of laser sights swung over the stills and equipment, seeking them in the dark. Bolan crouched behind a stack of pallets. Two of the stills were bleeding rivers of whiskey onto the distillery floor. Another shell hit the still Bolan had been using for cover. He watched as one of the growing lakes of alcohol caught fire.

Manning was twenty feet away behind a refrigeration unit. The dot of a laser sight crawled over his cover and a shotgun roared. Manning hunched as the door of the unit blew off its hinges. The corner of Bolan's cover exploded in splinters. Grimaldi stood behind a still and watched the burning pool creep toward him. He raised an eyebrow at Bolan pointedly.

The fire alarm suddenly started blaring throughout the distillery, and the overhead sprinklers rattled and hissed into life. Police and fire would be on their way if they weren't already.

Bolan assessed the situation quickly.

The assassins were using heavy machinery for cover. Bolan looked up at the banks of skylights lining the roof of the distilling floor. His machine pistols rolled in his hands as he drew twin lines of 9 mm rounds across the skylights. The windows shattered under the onslaught. Heavy glass fell through the rain of the sprinklers in glittering, deadly shards across the killer's positions.

Men in the back of the distillery screamed. They were wearing body armor, but they should have been wearing helmets and gloves as well.

Bolan ran forward to one of the stills. He dropped his weapons on their slings and took the ladder three rungs at a time. The Executioner crouched on the catwalk and took out another offensive grenade.

He pulled the pin and flung the grenade as he ran down the catwalk. The thump and boom of the enemy shotguns was eclipsed by the high-explosive thunder of the grenade. The Executioner came to the edge of the catwalk. The enemy was below him behind a pair of forklifts parked nose to nose. Bolan's suppressed weapons hissed in his hands as he went for head shots.

Grimaldi and Manning came around the stills, their weapons cycling in their hands.

Laurent Couvier screamed. His face was bloodied from the shower of broken glass. He and one of his surviving men hurled themselves between two heavily laden pallets.

Manning and Grimaldi stood and shot. The last two men behind the forklifts fell with their heads broken open to the sky.

Bolan crouched and reloaded. They had Courvier pinned. "Laurent! I want information! You come out now and you live!"

"Burn!" Laurent and his man popped up. Orange fire erupting as they emptied the high-explosive shells in their shotguns into the giant whiskey still Bolan crouched upon. "Burn, motherfucker!"

Flaming whiskey was slopping down the sides of the still out of a half dozen blasted orifices. Bolan was soaked through with it. The Executioner's eyes slitted as he scanned the pallet behind Courvier and his friend. It was stacked with metal barrels. The barrels had the universal hazardous chemical warning sticker on them. Beneath the stickers in bold block lettering was the chemical symbol for sulfuric acid.

Courvier fired two more rounds into the still and dropped back down. The whiskey was coming out in fiery streams. "Burn in hell!" Courvier screamed.

Bolan rose and sprayed his weapons. The barrels shuddered and burst their seams as Bolan burned sixty bullets into them.

Laurent Courvier and his associate screamed like the damned in hell as the barrels sprayed them with concentrated sulfuric acid.

Bolan slapped a fresh magazine into one of his weapons.

Courvier rose, twisting and screaming as the acid took effect. Bolan gave him a mercy shot. Manning put a bullet into the other man's temple and he fell dead on top of Courvier.

The ladder behind Bolan was on fire. He vaulted the guardrail and stepped into space. He bent his knees, but the jolt still ran from his heels to his skull as his boots hit the distillery floor. Grimaldi lifted his chin at the wall beneath the office. "Take a look at that."

Beneath the shattered office were two massive storage tanks on trailers. The markings on them said they were filled with gasoline.

Manning slid a fresh magazine into his weapon. "Acid and gas. They were getting ready to burn and bug out."

Bolan glanced at the door. The layout was simple. The raw materials came in the front. They were distilled, processed, bottled and stored and then came out the back for distribution. "Let's finish this."

Bolan kicked the door. The short hallway beyond was empty. Water from the sprinklers rained down, and the fire alarm honked on interminably. Bolan kicked in an office door to his right.

The office was a scene out of a nightmare.

The bodies of a man and woman lay on the floor, and Faye Ganzaga was stabbing them repeatedly. She turned in a killing frenzy and lunged for Bolan's throat.

Bolan's shot stopped her in her tracks.

Manning frowned at the butchered humans in the middle of the floor. "Those are the Russian scientists."

"Burn and bug out," Bolan stated. "They're not leaving any loose ends."

"So if Faye was here, doing..." Grimaldi looked at the bodies. "Then where's The Moor?"

At that same moment the door kicked off its hinges and slammed into Bolan.

The Moor charged through and piled into the Executioner with an immense revolver blazing in his hand.

Bolan and Gaultier Salamanca went down in a tangle of limbs as flames roared across the room at shoulder height. Bolan's gun hand slammed against the desk and his IDW was smashed from his grip. The Moor rammed the muzzle of his pistol into Bolan's side and squeezed the trigger. The soldier grimaced as he took the Magnum hammer blows and prayed for his armor to hold.

"Die you fuck!" The Moor screamed.

Guns were firing all around, and the higher pitched crack of a fragmentation grenade joined the cacophony.

Bolan jerked his head aside as The Moor tried to shoot him in the face. His eardrums compressed with the sound and muzzle-blast and unburned gunpowder seared his cheek. The Moor's eyes bugged as Bolan clamped his hands around his throat and cinched it tight. Bolan drew his knees up and planted both boots into The Moor's chest. He pushed out with all of his strength and hurled his adversary away.

Gaultier reeled. He pointed his .357 Magnum pistol at Bolan's face again. The soldier grabbed the IDW and took deadly aim and fired.

Bolan rolled up to one knee as The Moor fell to the carpet.

Grimaldi and Manning knelt in opposite corners of the room. The big Canadian came over in a crouch and peered in Bolan's eyes to see if he was all right. "Jack got the two who came in behind Gaultier. Then I fragged the hallway."

Bolan pushed himself to his feet, filling his other hand with his second machine pistol.

Grimaldi lifted his head. "I hear sirens."

Bolan shook his head and shoved out his jaw, yawning to try to make his ear pop. He couldn't hear much. "Let's move."

19

Lac Saint-Jean, Quebec

Lucky La Tuque Liquors had burned to the ground and Bolan and Daniela Antonetti stood among the ashes.

Manning and Grimaldi had pulled a fade while Bolan had stayed at the distillery with the suspects and the evidence. The RCMP had been ready to arrest him and throw away the key no matter what the Canadian Department of National Defence said, until Bolan had shown them the metal cylinders and the documents he'd discovered. Dr. Ferentinos had taken the cylinders to the mobile field lab and confirmed Bolan's find.

All six were full of live, highly mutated Group A Streptococcal Bacteria.

The RCMP confirmed that although Bolan had stopped The Moor's shipment, six cylinders were unaccounted for.

The Executioner suspected Grimaldi and Manning were already somewhere in the town of Alma, Quebec, but they had not made contact yet. RCMP Emergency Response Teams had been first to arrive on the scene and found the roadside liquor store that was to have taken the shipment in flames.

Every airport in Canada had soldiers and police screening the gates, but the running bets were that the cylinders of bacteria had left the country already.

"So it's gone." Sergeant Antonetti watched the blackened ashes drift in the afternoon breeze.

Every instinct Bolan had told him something was wrong. "Why here?"

"Probably because the Union Corse had a piece of this liquor store."

"I don't doubt that." Bolan glanced out across the blue waters. "But why up here? Why north? All the best smuggling routes would be down along the border with the U.S. where the cities are thick, or along the coasts."

Antonetti glanced at the pine-tree-laden horizon. "Well, Lac Saint-Jean empties into the Saguenay River, and that empties into the St. Lawrence. The St. Lawrence is a major smuggling route all the way from Newfoundland down to Lake Ontario. It's a little circuitous, but...maybe that's the point?"

Bolan stared into the ashes as if he could read them like tea leaves. He shook his head. "No."

"I don't see a northern connection," Antonetti said as she waved her arm to encompass the northern horizon. "You go far enough that way, and there's nothing staring back at you but black Arctic water and ice pack."

Bolan's phone rang. He stepped a few feet away and clicked it open. "Where are you?" he asked when he heard Manning's voice.

"We're in Alma. Where're you? Lucky La Tuque's?"

"Yeah."

"We saw that on the local news. What's the situation?"

"It's gone. The RCMP is hunting for the owners. You got a plane?"

"Yeah, Jack rented one and we flew to the airfield at Roberval. It's across the lake from Alma. Alma's got an airfield as well, so we have options. We arranged safehouses in both towns. You got a destination in mind?"

"Don't know yet. Be ready." Bolan clicked off the phone.

"There're cities on the Arctic Circle," Antonetti continued. "But I just don't see Middle Eastern terrorists coming to pick up a shipment at the North Pole."

"No, we have two different lots of bacteria. Two different customers. Two different destinations."

"Well..." The Mountie bit her lip in thought and gazed due north again. "Russia's straight thataway."

"The Russians wouldn't buy back their own bacteriological technology. They just come in, kill everyone and take it."

"The Chinese?"

"They might buy a live sample for study and then make their own, but barrels of the stuff? That implies a buyer who doesn't have the talent or technology to make his own." Bolan glanced away from the smoldering ruins of the not so Lucky La Tuque Liquor Emporium. His eyes narrowed as he looked northwest. "The Bering Strait would be the hard part. Both the United States and the Russians have listening posts there, and it's patrolled heavily on both sides."

Sergeant Antonetti cocked her head. "What?"

Bolan nodded to himself. "You'd need a specially modified boat, probably a diesel-electric coastal infiltrator. It would be a long, long haul and fraught with danger. They'd have to hug the coast of Alaska, crawling along the bottom. Once they got to the Canadian coastline it'd be easier. But they still need a port with an airfield to make the pickup."

Antonetti perked a bemused eyebrow. "You want to speak in English?"

Bolan pulled out his handheld computer and clicked it into geographic mode. A political-geographic representation of the planet spun on the screen.

Bolan worked the buttons and spun the globe until they were looking at the Arctic ice cap and the ring of continents and oceans surrounding it. Bolan pulled out his stylus. He tapped the Bering Strait between Russia and Alaska. "That's the gauntlet they have to run." He ran the stylus along the northernmost coast of Alaska and kept moving east along Canada.

Antonetti grinned. "You're in Nunavut now, buddy."

"That's right homegirl, and you're right. The bacteria is no longer in Quebec. It flew out of Roberval or Alma earlier today." Bolan clicked a button, and tiny outlines of airplanes appeared next to the cities of northernmost Canada. They were few and far between. "Here are your airstrips with regularly scheduled runs." He worked his way down the coast. "There's Inuvik, but you have to go down the Mackenzie Delta to get to it. That's dangerous for our friends, particularly in summer during the fishing season. They're best bet would be…"

Bolan dragged his stylus down the north coast of Canada and stopped on the next town with an airplane symbol. "Here."

The town's name was Kugluktuk.

"Okay…" Sergeant Antonetti stared at her hometown. "So who's bringing flesh-eating bacteria into my 'hood?"

"It's all conjecture at this point."

"Who!"

"The Union Corse is taking it there, that we know." Bolan clicked his personal computer shut. "But I'm betting a North Korean sub is coming to pick it up."

Kugluktuk, Nunavut

THE MIDNIGHT SUN HUNG low in the sky. Behind Bolan lay the treeless expanse of the Arctic tundra. Before him whitecaps rippled on the black water.

The RCMP had checked every flight coming and going from every airstrip in Nunavut. There were no unscheduled flights. No anomalous departures or arrivals. Nothing that in any way could be connected with the Union Corse. Bolan had been advised to go home by the RCMP.

The Executioner decided to take the long way home.

Sergeant Antonetti who had been granted leave due to her traumatic experience, was determined to go along for the ride.

Bolan picked up his gear as an ancient sky-blue pickup truck approached the outside of the air terminal. A blond woman in a leather jacket stuck her head out of the window and waved happily. "Hey, Dani! Who're the hunks, eh?"

"American secret agents," Antonetti replied, laughing.

Bolan threw his gear in the back of the truck. "Who's she?"

Antonetti tossed her bag in behind it. "That's Feli, the

other Swiss girl in Kugluktuk. She's a doctor at the clinic and teaches chemistry at the school."

Grimaldi and Manning climbed in the back of the truck while Bolan and Antonetti slid into the cab. Bolan had to lean his head forward so it wouldn't bang against the racked rifles. He held out a hand. "Cooper."

Feli ran her eyes up and down Bolan approvingly as she took his hand. "Felicitas."

It was midnight, but as they rode into town it looked like four o'clock in the afternoon. "Tell me, Feli. You seen any strangers around lately?" Bolan asked as they drove.

"Nothing unusual. Some fishermen, some hunters from lower down. There's an Inuit hunting party from the islands camping out on the other side of Sliding Hill by Coppermine River. They've been sticking to themselves, only came into town for some supplies from the Co-op once." Feli shrugged. "I think they're pretty tribal. Don't like townies."

Bolan filed that away.

Antonetti raised a warning eyebrow. "You hold that thought, Cowboy. You want to ask them if they've seen anything strange, you be respectful, and you go through me. Keep in mind that ninety percent of the population of Kugluktuk is Inuit. You pull one of your 'hard probes' on any natives, and I promise you, there will be hell to pay."

Bolan nodded. "Okay."

Antonetti looked surprised.

"Okay," Bolan repeated. "You grew up among these people. They're your friends and neighbors. We do it your way."

Feli pulled up to a log cabin. "Here you go. I opened it up and aired it out this morning after you called." She took two sets of keys from her pocket. "Ted and Thelma Aglooik are away, and they won't mind your friends squatting for a couple of days. Your Jeep's gassed up and in the garage. Once you settle and get some sleep you need to come into town. Everyone's excited to see you."

Antonetti was giddy with excitement. "Will do."

"Thanks for your help," Bolan said.

Feli grinned and waved. "See you boys later!" She hopped into her truck, shouting out the window as she pulled away. "Welcome to Kugluktuk!"

"Nice girl," Manning observed. "I like her."

Grimaldi dropped his bag. "So how do you want to play it?"

Bolan looked at his watch. His team was done in. They had taken a hell of a beating in the past seventy-two hours, spending the last fourteen of them hopping from airstrip to airstrip across Canada. They were near the Arctic Circle and fresh out of leads. "We'll sack out for a few hours. Then Dani checks in with the RCMP station and we start respectfully poking around."

The Mountie smiled. "Shouldn't we be on the buddy system?"

"Right, you guys take the Algooik's cabin. Dani, you're with me."

Manning and Grimaldi didn't say a word. Their smirks spoke volumes.

Bolan followed Antonetti into the log cabin where she had been raised. It took less than a minute to sweep the four small rooms, the cellar and the loft. Bolan smiled. "I think we're safe, for the moment."

"After what I went through..." Her shoulders twitched with revulsion as she barred the door. "You're never too safe."

"That's why there's the buddy system."

"Everybody needs a buddy." Her clothes began forming a pile on the polar bear skin rug at her feet.

Bolan ran his eyes over her body while the late-night sun filtered through the curtains and lit the room. "You sure this is wise?" he asked her.

"I learned my lesson."

"What was that again?"

Her smile turned predatory as she draped her arms around Bolan's neck and pressed her curves against him. "Always sleep with the International Man of Mystery."

20

Bolan opened his eyes. IT was four o'clock in the morning, and the sun was shining softly. But something more than that was wrong. Bolan spoke into Antonetti's ear. "Wake up."

The Mountie made a sleepy noise and snuggled deeper into the blankets.

"There's someone in the house."

Antonetti's eyes flew open, instantly lucid. Her pistol came out from under her pillow. Bolan rolled out of the bed with a pistol in either hand.

They stood like naked statues, extending all of their senses and listening.

Nothing was moving, but alarm bells were ringing up and down Bolan's spine. He flung the bedroom door open and stepped aside. No hail of bullets came. He slid out of the bedroom, covering the living area and the kitchen. Antonetti shadowed him.

The front door was still barred. From where he stood the windows still appeared to be locked.

Antonetti lowered her pistol. "Unless they dug a tunnel into the cellar, I don't see—"

Bolan turned toward the loft, his pistols swinging up to the hatch in the ceiling. An Inuit man dropped down from the hatchway nearly on top of Antonetti. A second killer dropped down behind him. Antonetti screamed as the huge skinning knife sliced across her forearm and her pistol fell from her hand. She whirled, and her spinning heel kick clouted the killer across the jaw. The man took the shot and countered with his own spinning kick. Antonetti was smashed to the floor.

The Beretta 93-R machine pistol strobed fire in Bolan's hand, walking a 3-round burst up the killer's torso. The man behind him flung his butcher blade at Bolan's head. The Executioner jerked aside as the knife flashed past and sank into a beam. The killer moved quickly, drawing a hunting revolver with a scope from underneath his jacket.

The man gasped as Bolan's 3-round burst tore through his right thigh. Bolan's second burst ripped through the man's other thigh and dropped him sitting back on his heels. The soldier strode forward. The slide of the Desert Eagle cracked across the man's left cheek. Bolan whipped the big gun back and laid the assassin's right cheek open to the bone with a vicious backhand. Blood flew as Bolan followed up with his left, whipping the still smoking Beretta machine pistol beneath the killer's chin in an ugly uppercut.

The man collapsed to the carpet.

"Striker!" Manning was shouting outside the door.

"We're okay!" Bolan kept the Beretta trained on the hatch and unlocked the door. "But the house isn't clear!"

Grimaldi came in with his MAC-10 leveled. Bolan nodded at the open hatch. Manning stuck his head in the door and went outside again.

Bolan grabbed his medical kit. Antonetti's hand was white-knuckled around her forearm but blood was welling up between her fingers. "You all right?"

"I'm gonna need stitches."

"Clear!" Manning's head peaked down out of the hatch "They jimmied the loft window."

Bolan put a field dressing on Antonetti's arm. The wound was deep and ugly, but she could still wiggle her fingers. Bolan was betting no nerves had been cut.

She smiled weakly. "We'd better put some clothes on. Rudi's gonna be here any minute, and he's not going to like this."

Bolan applied another field dressing as the first one bled through. "Who's Rudi?"

"My ex-boyfriend."

SERGEANT RUDI SILA INUA was not happy. The Inuit was a tall, lanky man in a blue RCMP windbreaker, jeans and boots. He wore a .44 Magnum Ruger openly in a cross-draw holster on the front of his belt. Across the room, Feli was sewing up Antonetti's arm, but it was the other patient who held everyone's attention.

The surviving assassin lay strapped to a gurney awaiting his medical flight to the hospital in Yellowknife. His elevated legs were swathed in bandages and IVs hung out of both arms. His long hair was disheveled and his face was badly and swollen. Both of his wrists were handcuffed to the frame.

Bolan turned to Sila Inua. "Sergeant, is this guy local?"

"Nope." The RCMP officer shook his head. "Never seen him." Sila Inua spoke a few words in Inuktituk.

The prisoner stared into the middle-distance in stone-faced silence.

The sergeant stared back. *"Parlez-vous français?"*

Across the room Feli was putting her twelfth suture into Antonetti's arm. The Mountie ignored the procedure and watched the interrogation. She held an ice pack against the massive purple lump along her jaw and cheek. "Rudi, you think he's Métis?"

"Not sure he's even Inuit." Sila Inua turned his laconic gaze on Bolan. "Hard to tell with his face all beat up like that."

Bolan shrugged.

The sergeant glanced back at the prisoner. "Might be he's Innu, but if he is, he's a long way from home, and I don't speak none of that."

Bolan examined the suspect critically. They had cut away his sleeves to administer the IVs. The man's forearms were corded muscle. Despite his wounded and medicated condition, his physique appeared to be carved out of solid rock. He'd eaten Antonetti's round kick without blinking and had hit her back with one that had left her half-conscious on the floor.

"You mind if I have a try?" Bolan asked.

Sila Inua grunted noncommittally.

Bolan stood in front of the prisoner. The man stared through him. The Executioner spoke quietly.

The prisoner's eyes flew wide with shock.

Bolan's suspicions were confirmed.

"Jeez!" Sila Inua stared at Bolan incredulously. "You speak Innu?"

"No." Bolan glanced back at the prisoner. The man's

arms flexed against his handcuffs. His face was flushed with rage. "But I can swear a bit in Korean."

"Korean?" Sila Inua was shocked.

"He's North Korean Special Purpose Force, Reconnaissance Brigade. My bet is he's from one of the infiltration detachments."

Sergeant Sila Inua frowned deeply. "He's a long way from home, eh?"

"Most North Korean infiltrators are trained for cross-border actions in South Korea. But they also have their Foreign Clandestine Operation Units, made up of North Koreans who can physically pass for Chinese, Japanese or South East Asians. They're given intensive linguistic and cultural training. Their usual missions are abduction and assassination."

Sila Inua sipped coffee, but his right hand had unconsciously come to rest on the butt of his pistol. "Still, a long way from home."

"Yeah, but the rumor's always been that they have a cadre who can pass as North American Arctic aboriginals."

Sila Inua raised a disbelieving eyebrow.

"Their primary mission is believed to be cutting the Alaskan oil pipelines and sabotaging the U.S. and Canada's northernmost military bases."

The man on the gurney glared at Bolan.

Bolan nodded. "He understands every word we're saying. He speaks probably some Inuktituk and French. The infiltration operatives are highly trained, motivated, and absolutely loyal to the North Korean regime. They're the best of the best. The only reason he gave himself away is morphine, shock and blood loss, and that was only a facial expression. He won't talk without an extensive regimen of interrogation and torture."

The prisoner's face tightened at the word torture and he resumed staring into the distance.

Antonetti sighed. "So we're out of leads, again?"

"No, he and his friend were here and they tried to take us down. That tells me the bacteria is still in Canada and they're waiting on the sub to take it out. Our friend is here to plug any leaks and stop or divert any lines of investigation."

"Jeez…" Sila Inua stared at Bolan with grudging respect. "You're good."

"The bad news is I think you have at least a squad of his friends camping out behind the sliding hill."

"Jesus Christ!"

Everyone looked up at the sound of thunder. Feli screamed as bullets shattered the clinic windows.

Tracers streaked overhead, drawing smoking lines through the infirmary. Bolan flicked his phone to walkie-talkie mode. "Gary, where are you?"

"Taking fire, Striker! They hit Dani's cabin with some kind of shoulder-launched weapon. It's gone. We were in the Algooik house. We bugged out the back. Making our way toward you!"

Thunder rolled across Kugluktuk a second time.

Sila Inua grimaced. "What the hell is that? A howitzer?"

Bolan smelled the wind blowing in through the shattered windows. The acrid smell of high explosive was mixed with the burning vaporous stench of gas. "I'd say it was a fuel-air explosion."

"What the hell does that mean?"

"It means we have to get out of here right now," Bolan said.

Antonetti drew her pistol. "I hear shooting out back."

They were pinned down and about to get blown up.

"I need a rifle," Bolan shouted.

"Here!" Feli had unlocked a cabinet and pulled out a Remington Safari rifle. "Take it!"

Bolan caught the big game gun. It was a .458 Winchester Magnum. It had been designed specifically with African water buffaloes and elephants in mind.

"We had a polar bear come into the infirmary once!" Felix explained.

Bolan checked the action. There were three rounds in the magazine and three more sausage-sized cartridges in a leather cuff sewn around the stock. Bolan flicked his Beretta to single shot and tossed it to Feli.

"Cover me!"

Bolan burst out the emergency-room door. Handguns fired from the shattered infirmary windows as Bolan hit the dirt, rolling Sila Inua's Toyota 4x4 behind. Bullets swarmed into the side of the vehicle.

Bolan could see Manning and Grimaldi half a block down behind a pickup. Both men were engaging the shooters across the street from Bolan.

Across the street a man with a four-foot metal tube across his shoulder was taking aim at the clinic. He dropped down behind a car when he saw Bolan. The Executioner lowered his aim slightly and fired.

The rifle kicked into Bolan's shoulder like a mule.

The rocketeer hurtled backward with his rib cage in exploded ruin. The muzzle of his weapon tilted skyward. Fire blasted out of the launch tube fore and aft as his fingers clamped on the trigger assembly. He disappeared in fire as the rocket wash blasted into the ground and expanded around him. The men around him screamed as the flames enveloped them. The infantry rocket screamed skyward trailing smoke and fire.

"Cover!" Bolan roared.

Grimaldi and Manning dived through the doors of the barbershop. Bolan watched the rocket apex and tip over as its motor burned out. Some of the citizens of Kugluktuk were beginning to stick their heads out of windows to see what had touched off World War III in their hamlet. Bolan lunged into Sila Inua's truck and hit the loudspeaker.

"Stay in your homes! I repeat! Stay in your homes!"

Storm shutters and heavy doors began slamming up and down the street.

Bolan leaped out of the truck and dived for the clinic doors as the spent rocket fell to Earth.

Every remaining window shattered inward as the blast hit. The lights went out and the infirmary shuddered down to its foundations. Everything not bolted to the floor or a wall toppled or took flight.

The world was suddenly utterly still.

Bolan disentangled himself and came to his feet, jacking a fresh cartridge into the safari rifle. The light fixtures hung from the ceiling shattered and sparking. What was left of the fire suppression sprinklers spit water in fits and starts from the twisted spigots. Sila Inua had grabbed Feli and Antonetti and shoved them into lockers. They spilled out with their pistols leveled. The infirmary doors had been ripped from their hinges and blown into pieces. A jagged four-foot wooden shard lay embedded in the locker next to the one Feli had taken cover in. Another three-foot chunk had sunk into their suspect from his navel to his chest like a giant wooden cleaver. Feli checked his pulse and shook her head.

Bolan stepped into the reception area. The front wall and the ceiling were gone. Two blackened sagging walls formed a smoking shell that was open to the blue sky above.

Bolan crossed the street. The blackened bodies of the assassins were barely discernable in the twisted wreckage of the cars. He spotted a broken but recognizable Russian-made A-91 compact assault rifle. Bolan nodded to himself. The North Koreans had a thriving small arms business, but most of it was very low tech. For the high-tech and clandestine stuff they shopped in the former Soviet Union.

Sila Inua came out, scowling at the remnants of his ruined truck. He reached into the smoldering cab and pulled out a battered rifle. He checked the action and nodded.

Manning and Grimaldi emerged from the shattered barbershop.

"Sergeant, how did that hunting party arrive?"

"By boat."

"How many?"

"Twelve, thirteen maybe."

"There were five in front and they're accounted for. Say four or five in back and maybe two or three in camp. I'd make it seven or eight still effective and extracting."

"They came in on an old Boston whaler. If they try putting out to sea, I can put half a dozen boats in the water all filled with men with rifles."

"They won't go out to sea. They'll go south, down the Coppermine River and extract into the interior. It's a hundred miles to the tree line. These men will have been extensively trained to not only look and act like Inuit but to survive and live like them in the wilderness.

Feli's truck screeched to a halt in front of them. It had been parked around the side of the clinic, but the blast wave had still blown out all her windows and her headlights. Antonetti was in the passenger seat. Grimaldi and Manning trotted across the street and jumped in the back. Bolan slapped the top of the cab as he and Sila Inua jumped in the bed. "Coppermine River! Hit it!"

The truck spit gravel as Feli floored it.

Bolan leaned out over the passenger window. "Hand out those rifles!"

Antonetti reached back to the rack and handed out a Winchester 30-30 and an old .303 Lee-Enfield while the truck lurched up the sliding hill. Bolan took the ancient scope sighted rifle and opened the action. Ten rounds were loaded in the clip.

They crested the hill to find the Coppermine River snaking south. A cluster of abandoned tents surrounded a still smoking campfire. Down river a blue and white boat was motoring inland.

There were seven men in the boat. All except the pilot turned to face their pursuers. All had short automatic rifles in their hands. The range was still long for the short-range assault weapons the Koreans carried, but they would cut Feli's truck to pieces when they closed in. Bolan hit the cab with his fist.

"Stop!"

The truck fishtailed in the sand and gravel by the river.

Bolan slung the old Lee-Enfield and took up the elephant rifle. It wasn't a long-range weapon either. Hitting a man-sized, moving target with it would be problematic.

A boat, however, presented a much more tempting target.

"Take cover."

Bolan's team bailed out of the truck. The Executioner took cover behind the cab as the Koreans opened up. Bolan took careful aim at the back of the boat near the waterline. The express rifle roared. Upriver the boat suddenly swerved. Bolan dropped behind the truck as a hail of rifle fire hit it.

He was rewarded by the sound of the boat's engine revving up to a broken scream of overdrive and then dying. For a moment all gunfire ceased. Bolan dropped the elephant gun and took up the antique. The others had taken cover in a rock formation by the bank.

The enemy was adrift with a shattered engine, and their boat was slowly returning back downriver toward the sea, and Bolan's team.

All of them began unloading their weapons at once at the shoreline.

Bolan heard the hollow sound of a 40 mm grenade launcher and broke cover. He threw himself down as the cab of Feli's truck came apart in a spray of glass and shrapnel behind him. He rolled up in a sniper's sit, one leg folded beneath him, his other forming a rest for his elbow.

The enemy grenadier came into sharp focus in the telescopic sight. He had just slapped a munition down the smoking black muzzle of the launcher mounted beneath his assault weapon. He took a fatal second to adjust his ladder sight.

The old Lee-Enfield bucked into Bolan's shoulder, and the grenadier's throat blossomed into bloody rags as the blunt-nosed hunting bullet blasted through his neck. The infiltrator flopped forward over the rail and plunged into the river.

Bolan had already flicked his bolt and chambered another round. The rifle roared, and his second shot shattered the sternum of another Korean and knocked him to the bottom of the boat. The Executioner rolled behind a rock as tracers tore the ground a few feet away.

As a unit the Koreans leaped over the far side of the boat and disappeared.

"They're using the boat for cover!" Manning ripped a burst into the boat to keep the Koreans honest.

"Be ready!" Bolan said. He took careful aim at the boat right by the waterline and fired.

A black hole appeared in the white, fiberglass hull. Bolan shifted his aim and fired again.

A moment later a body drifted facedown in the water from behind the stern. Bolan kept his aim on the boat.

The body in the water shuddered as Manning put a burst into it to make sure. "I make that four hostiles remaining," he said.

The remaining infiltrators suddenly breached out of the water in pairs like vengeful river spirits. They had ducked beneath the boat and swum through the dark water to bring themselves to the riverbank and close to their enemies.

Time seemed to slow as everyone began firing at once.

Sila Inua fell as a burst walked up his chest.

Grimaldi and Manning cut the man down. Antonetti shot the assassin next to him three times in the face and dropped him into the shallows. The elephant rifle thundered in Bolan's hands and the killer closest to him was hammered in ruins back beneath the water.

Bolan dropped the spent express rifle and slapped leather for his Desert Eagle as the remaining killer swung his rifle muzzle toward Bolan's head.

The man jerked as a rifle bullet smashed into his back between his shoulder blades. His head snapped back as Bolan's bullet crushed his skull a second later. Feli knelt with a smoking hunting rifle in her hands, still covering the dead man.

Bolan nodded in thanks. "I owe you one."

Antonetti knelt beside Sila Inua. He lay on the ground gasping and blinking in shock. She tore open his shirt and nodded. "Thank God."

Sergeant Sila Inua was wearing his vest, and the bright copper bases of five bullets protruded out of the white Kevlar fabric.

Bolan stared at the bullet-riddled boat as it drifted by. The bacteria canisters wouldn't be in it, nor would they be in the infiltrator camp.

They were gone.

But the fact that the North Koreans were still in Kugluktuk meant they hadn't received orders to extract yet. There would be a radio in the boat and probably one in camp. They would have sent out a message that the attack on the clinic had failed and they were extracting inland.

Extracting inland would have been Plan B, and an emergency measure.

Plan A would have been quietly extracting out to sea.

"The infiltrators came in by normal means, probably through Alaska. They had a week or two to buy a boat and come along the coast. They wouldn't risk the same route going back. They were going to go straight out to sea. In a Boston whaler they wouldn't have a lot of range. Someone was going to pick them up, probably by air."

Antonetti looked north. "Straight shot, it's a hundred miles to Cambridge Island across the gulf. But there's nothing there other than the towns of Holman on the west side and Cambridge Bay on the east, and that's three hundred miles over empty tundra, both ways."

"Right," Bolan said. "But both towns have airstrips, don't they?"

"They do."

Manning scratched his jaw. "You think Renoir and his boys are hiding in town?"

"No, too much of a splash. They would be strangers in small towns that are almost entirely Inuit. They'd be too recognizable."

Grimaldi frowned. "Well, Jesus, Sarge, there's only about a thousand islands between here and the North Pole."

"Not with airstrips."

Antonetti sighed. "You just said they wouldn't be hiding in a town, and these are Mafia scumbags, city boys. They aren't living in tents on some island."

"No, they're not," Bolan agreed. "They're someplace they feel safe. Someplace they control. Someplace they can actually hide if the authorities show up."

Manning shrugged. "Where the hell do French gangsters find that in the Arctic Circle?"

Sila Inua sat up painfully, but his eyes were focused like a hawk. "You go to the goddamn, northernmost thing in the world."

Bolan pulled his personal computer from his jacket and snapped it open, clicking it into map mode. "Show me."

21

"Borden Island dead ahead!" Jack Grimaldi squinted, red-eyed and exhausted, across the gleaming Arctic waters beneath their plane. They had been flying for twelve hours, circuitously, tortuously, hopping their way from island to island, airfield to airfield. Canada was the second largest country on earth and the least densely populated.

On a straight shot, Borden Island was eight hundred miles almost due north of Kugluktuk, but it was a classic situation of you couldn't get there from here. They'd been forced to fly a sixteen hundred mile arc of airfields within range of the Cessna Air Ambulance plane.

Their objective was finally in sight.

Sergeants Antonetti and Sila Inua had been ordered to wait for RCMP Emergency Response Teams from Yellowknife, but Bolan had decided they couldn't wait. He told the Mounties they'd have to physically stop him or order Canadian Military jets to shoot down his team.

Antonetti and Sila Inua had broken orders to go with him. Feli had volunteered. Initially Bolan had balked, but he needed every crack rifleman and -woman he could get his hands on.

Bolan shrugged into his harness. One of Kugluktuk's

claims to fame was that it had the second northernmost skydiving club in the world and they had commandeered parachutes. Only Russia had a club higher up, and they catered to the military. They had also stocked up on hunting rifles, pistols and shotguns from the citizens of Kugluktuk. With Feli's help they had borrowed the life-flight medical plane that had been waiting for the now perished Korean infiltrator. They had taken off within an hour of the battle of Coppermine River.

Bolan looked at his team.

Antonetti had jumped before. Sila Inua and Feli hadn't. They would land in the plane with Grimaldi, probably into a hot landing zone. Bolan, Manning and Antonetti would mount the airborne assault and try to secure the LZ. So far the enemy had produced two flamethrowers and a rocket flame projector. God only knew what kind of life insurance they were packing on Borden Island.

The mission was ugly all the way around.

"Goddamn it!" Grimaldi snarled around the Thermos of coffee he'd been nursing. "Sarge! Look at this!"

Bolan took out his binoculars and sat in the copilot seat. He scanned the coast of Borden Island. As they approached the Northern Lights Mine, Bolan could see there were three long, very low buildings with a crimson and white Canadian flag painted across the roofs. The harbor was a concrete fortress built to survive the Arctic ice pack making a fist around it and then breaking in the summer heat.

In the harbor was the unmistakable cigar shape of a surfaced submarine.

Ant-sized people and their cargo were loading into the black boat.

Bolan grimaced. "Plan B! We hit the sub! Right now!"

BOLAN DROPPED HIS TOGGLES and reached for his guns. He ignored the men loading supplies onto the sub from the dinghy and leveled his pistols at the man coming up out of the abbreviated sail with a rifle. Bolan's pistols blazed in his hands. Plummeting through space did not make for a very stable firing position and sparks flew off the sail around the rifleman. Bolan dropped the Desert Eagle and took his Beretta 93-R in both hands. He flicked the selector to 3-round-burst mode and the Italian pistol began ripping off 3-round strings.

The Korean sailor jerked as his hip was shattered by one burst and the second ripped through his shoulders and neck. Bolan dropped the Beretta and took his steering toggles as he began to drift off target.

Another sailor stared in frozen horror a split second too long as Bolan descended. The Executioner drew his knees into his chest and planted both boots into the crewman as he stalled his chute. The crewman was sent flying into the Arctic Ocean.

Bolan slammed into the sub's steel deck plates with bone-jarring force.

A man ran up swinging a gaff. Bolan jerked his head aside as the steel hook struck sparks off of the deck and rammed his boot up between the sailor's legs. Bolan shoved the vomiting sailor aside and pulled a hunting pistol from his belt. He shot two sailors and a rifleman coming up from the sail.

Gary Manning went flying past Bolan far too quickly. "Shit!" The Canadian's boots slid along the slick side hull of the sub. The wind had his chute and he was dragged over the side into the water.

Behind Bolan, Antonetti hit the top deck hard. Bolan ran to the sail and shot a third rifleman struggling to get himself and his weapon up the narrow hatchway. He stuck his pistol down the hatch and shot into the interior. Bolan jerked back as weapons below answered and tracers streaked up from the hatch. The hull beneath Bolan vibrated as the diesels rumbled into life. He shot a look back.

Manning was treading water, trying to shrug out of his weapons and parachute before they pulled him under. "Go!" Manning shouted as he gulped seawater and hacked.

Gunfire was ripping up from the hatch in a crescendo, and from below Bolan could hear a man barking a single word again and again with the unmistakable authority of command. Bolan didn't need a translation. The man shouting below was the captain, and his order was clear.

"Dive! Dive! Dive!"

The water around the sub roiled and foamed as the submersible took on ballast.

Bolan pulled the pin on a fragmentation grenade and hurled it into the sub. The grenade detonated with a reverberating whipcrack and men screamed as the shrapnel expanded to fill the cramped compartment.

Bolan slid down the ladder and hit the bridge in a crouch, a .44 Magnum pistol clasped in both hands. The communications officer slumped dead in his chair, the left side of his face a bloody wasteland of shrapnel wounds. His sidearm was still in his hand.

Bolan spied the six green metal cylinders sitting on a pallet in the middle of the bridge.

Bullets ricocheted, striking sparks and shredding instruments as the surviving crewmen on the bridge all began shooting at once. The Executioner hunched behind the sail's bulkhead. He tensed as cold water slopped down the sail on top of him and continued flooding downward in a steady waterfall.

The hatch was open and the submarine was submerging.

Antonetti dropped halfway down the ladder tube. She yanked the hatch down and spun the wheel. Bolan whipped around the bulkhead and snapped off a shot. The nearly flat-headed .44 Magnum bullet ripped through the captain's body just beneath the rib cage, erupting out his back and taking most of his shredded liver and left kidney with it. He shuddered like a squid and fell dying to the deck.

Two crewmen ran forward screaming revenge for their late captain, their folding bayonets fixed. They fired their rifles dry and charged around the bulkhead. Bolan blocked a bayonet thrust at his face with the six-inch barrel of his revolver and jammed the muzzle up against the side of one man's chin and pulled the trigger. The Korean's mandible disappeared. Bolan squeezed his trigger a second time ending the man's agony.

The other man howled and thrust past his collapsing comrade. Steel burned along Bolan's side. The Executioner twisted to one side and rammed the smoking muzzle of his revolver into the sailor's left ear. The revolver detonated in Bolan's hand. The ensign's rifle fell from his grip.

Bolan shoved the brainless ensign aside. "Dani, are you all right?"

Antonetti slid down the ladder the rest of the way and ducked into the tiny alcove. "I think so."

"Cover me." Spotting Lorenzo Renoir, the Executioner dived into the bridge area. The .44 Magnum revolver thudded and blasted out the sonar screen by Renoir's head. Antonetti leaned around the bulkhead firing her pistol. Bolan could hear more men shouting from the front of the submarine and the pounding of feet in the corridor. He dropped the spent gun and drew the last pistol he'd commandeered in Kugluktuk. The deck was littered with the dead and wounded. Renoir and Bruno Sedin had taken cover near the front of the compartment.

The bridge was too narrow and too cramped to charge them, and Bolan was fresh out of hand grenades. He knew more Koreans would arrive and hit them in a rush. Bolan only had six bullets left.

He couldn't hold the bridge.

Bolan popped up. "Dani! Out the back! Move!" He fired three times to keep the enemies' heads down as Antonetti ran at a crouch through the bridge. She made for the rear door and dived through it. Instantly she was up, her pistol barking in her hand. "Move!"

Bolan ran for the door. He turned as men came screaming onto the bridge with rifles blazing. Renoir and Sedin rose, shooting. The Executioner turned, extended his pistol and pulled the trigger three times.

The pressurized bacteria containment cylinders burst like steel balloons. Bolan slammed the hatch and spun the wheel.

BIG DAMAGE RAISED his mighty arms toward the ceiling in rage. "Fuck!" he screamed as reality sunk in.

Renoir stared in disbelief at the leaking canisters. The blissfully unaware Korean crewmen were angrily yanking on the rear hatch. Submarine doors were made to bolt on either side to contain flooding compartments. It would take a blowtorch to burn through.

Consolata came onto the bridge with her little pistol in her hand. "What the hell is going on in... Oh... my...God..." Her voice trailed off in horror.

"That's right, Baby doll!" Sedin's hand clamped around her face. "We're dead!"

22

"You think that's all of them?" Antonetti lowered her pistol. Bolan held a smoking rifle he had taken from the armory compartment. The engineer and his assistant lay dead on the floor of the engine room. The two Koreans had come at them with a spanning wrench and a claw hammer, and Bolan and Antonetti had burned them down. The lone man in the galley had charged their guns with a cleaver.

The crew of the *Flawless Victory* wasn't giving up its boat without a fight.

"Yeah." Bolan nodded slowly and folded his bayonet. There was only one door into the engine room. They had cleared their side of the sub. The engine room was the end of the line. "We're safe for—"

"Jesus!" Antonetti nearly fell as the sub lurched. Bolan caught her by the waist and grabbed an overhead cleat as the deck tilted precipitously beneath their feet. Everything that wasn't nailed down fell over or slid across the engine room floor toward the door. "What was that?"

Bolan listened to the hull rumble. His eyes flared as gunfire echoed hollowly through the metal hull from the forward compartments. Bolan's eyes slowly closed to slits. "The crew is doing my job for me."

Antonetti stared at Bolan uncertainly. "What do you mean?"

"I couldn't let this submarine get to North Korea. So I let the bacteria out of containment."

"I know." She swallowed with difficulty. "We're a plague ship."

"That's right. This submarine and the bacteria on board can never see the surface. Some of the crew must have known what they were carrying. The crew would be dead before they ever reached the Korean Peninsula, and they can't allow any evidence of North Korea's involvement in buying weapons of mass destruction from the Union Corse."

"So..." she paled. "We're going down."

Bolan took a long breath and let it out. "I'm sorry."

Antonetti looked away. She was silent for several long moments. "No...don't. Don't be sorry. You told me not to come. I came anyway. I'm a sergeant in the RCMP. My duty is clear. Containing the bacteria is my number one priority. I knew when I joined the force I might have to lay down my life in the line of duty...." She gazed around at the cold gray walls of the compartment despairingly. "But not like...this."

Bolan took her in his arms. "I know."

Antonetti was suddenly ripped from Bolan's arms screaming. The lights went black and Bolan flew against the bulkhead with bone-breaking force. Stars pulsed behind his eyes as his skull bounced against unyielding steel. Automatic alarms began to ring throughout the dying sub. The sub screamed in tearing, ripping agony. The hull howled and rippled like an earthquake.

Then just as suddenly the hull's screaming came to a stop.

Bolan lay still for a moment, waiting for the black Arctic depths to engulf him.

Instead, lurid, red light flickered, clicked and then stabilized as the emergency generator kicked in. Bolan groaned as he rolled to one knee and reached out for Antonetti. She was curled in a ball, clutching her bleeding nose. He gathered her into his arms as she wept and shook with adrenaline reaction. She rocked back and forth in his embrace.

"What…the fuck…was that?"

Bolan peered suspiciously at the ceiling. A thin, pressurized stream of water was spritzing into the engine compartment, but he couldn't be sure if it was a broken pipe or whether the pressure hull had been degraded.

"I think we hit bottom," he said.

"Bottom?"

"I don't know." Bolan watched the water spraying from above. For the moment it didn't seem to be getting worse. "My mental map of the Arctic Ocean floor is pretty vague, but ocean floor geography is like the rest of the planet. There are mountains and valleys, chasms and plains. We've come to rest on something."

Antonetti pushed her hand across the tears staining her face. "How deep?"

Bolan listened to the battered hull pop and tick with the pressure. "I don't know. We're in a small sub, and we were already underway with ballast tanks full and the engines steaming when the ship started to dive." Bolan tried to do the math with an incomplete equation. "We dived for less than minute. I'd say we're five hundred yards down at least, but less than a thousand. I don't know the specs of this sub, but it's made for coastal infiltration, not deep oceangoing. Anything much more than a thousand feet, fifteen hundred at the most, and she'd crack like an egg. We're above crush depth, that's all I can tell you."

Bolan omitted mentioning that crush depth could alter drastically for a submarine whose pressure hull had bounced off the bottom.

"So…we're safe?"

"We're okay." Bolan judged the deck was tilted at forty-five degrees. "For the moment."

"What about the rest of the crew?"

"Don't know. We haven't heard anything in a while. But we survived the crash, so we have to assume anyone who survived the gunfight did too."

"So…what do we do?"

Bolan wasn't sure he had any kind of answer.

23

Antonetti started and Bolan tensed at the sudden sound. The stricken submarine had continuously moaned, groaned and creaked like a haunted house since it had hit bottom, but this sound was new. It was the unmistakable thin, high echo of a woman's scream.

"Who was that?"

"I think there could only be one woman on this sub besides you," Bolan said.

"Consolata Malatesta."

"That would be my guess. She threw in her lot with the Union Corse after I hit her Family. It makes sense that she would bug out with them and let things cool down in North America for a while."

"What do you think made her— Jesus!" Antonetti started again as the crack of a gunshot reverberated through the hull.

Bolan listened to the echo fade. "I think someone on the other side of the sub just took the easy way out."

They were both silent.

They both looked up as a repetitive, mechanical clanking noise began hammering through the hull.

"You turned the engines off, right?"

Bolan frowned and listened. "Yeah."

"So what's that?" Antonetti shivered. "The air pump going?"

"No, someone's pounding on the hull."

Her hand went to her pistol. "You think they're trying to break into our side of the sub?"

"They'd need explosives, a welding torch, or an anti-armor weapon to get through the door to the bridge."

"Then what is it?"

"They're screwing it up, but it sounds like Morse code."

"They're sending out an SOS, hoping someone is listening?"

"Yeah." Bolan nodded as the signaler got it right. Whoever it was in the front of sub pounded out three quick clanks, three longer spaced ones, and three quick ones again. "They're sending out a Mayday."

They listened to the clank of the distress call being pounded by hand out into the black Arctic depths again and again.

BOLAN OPENED HIS EYES. The lights had dimmed and the sub was getting noticeably colder. The batteries were beginning to die. The air had begun to take on an unhealthy metallic tang. He looked up toward the hatch of the crewmen's quarters. Every compartment had a light mounted by the door. The lights were air-mixture indicators. The little light over the door was inexorably turning from orange to red.

The air mixture was going out of tolerance.

He wasn't sure how much time had passed but by his estimation they should have at least two days. But the sub had hit bottom hard and taken damage. They had already opened the emergency air cylinders on their side of the sub, and they lay in a spent pile in the corner. Bolan considered his options.

He could go forward, through the bridge, and see if he could scavenge any emergency air cylinders or scuba tanks for a few more hours of air.

Then again, he could do nothing.

Antonetti was asleep in his arms. There was a good chance she might have the mercy of simply not waking up as she slowly slipped into carbon-dioxide narcosis. It was better than anything else that might lie in store for her.

Failing either, there was always the gun.

Antonetti stirred as the clanging against the hull resumed. "God, isn't he dead yet?"

The frantic SOS had gone on almost continuously for hours and then fallen silent.

"Actually?" Bolan cocked his head. "I think he is."

"Then what—"

"Shh." Bolan listened. "It's Morse code, but it isn't an SOS." Bolan sat up from their nest. "It's coming from outside the sub."

"Oh my God!" Antonetti shot up. "What are they saying?"

Bolan held up his hand as the taps and thuds of the Morse letters pounded against the steel.

Bolan rose and grabbed his rifle as the message repeated itself. He began rapidly pounding the steel buttplate against the bulkhead. He took a deep breath and hammered his final message.

Antonetti took a deep breath. "You told them to stay away, didn't you?"

Bolan nodded. "I did."

The thudding continued. Antonetti shook her head. "What's he saying now?"

"They have a vaccine. They've come to get us out." Bolan allowed himself a sigh of relief. "We're going to make it."

Antonetti almost collapsed.

Bolan steadied her as the tapping continued. He listened for long moments. "The diver is saying their recovery vehicle's docking collar won't fit over the forward diver delivery compartment. We're going to have to go to the bridge and extract from the sail."

Antonetti nodded. "If they have a vaccine, then let's get the hell out of here."

They made their way back to the bridge. Bolan shot the bolt and drew his pistol. "I'm pretty sure everyone from the bridge forward is dead, but be ready."

She drew her pistol as Bolan swung the door open.

The bridge was a wax museum of horror. The deck was strewed with the corpses of crewman. Most of them had obviously died of bloody gunshot wounds. Those were the lucky ones. A Korean crewman lay wadded in a ball by the helm, his flesh chewed away from his body like leprosy gone mad. Another crewman lay near the communications console, he looked nearly normal save that his eyes had been eaten out of their sockets. They stared up blackly, the bacteria having devoured everything behind them as well.

Consolata Malatesta sat slumped by the ladder to the

sail. A small, faded string of purple bullae vesicles on her left cheek marred her perfect beauty with the telltale signs of the flesh-eating infection. Her hands were bloodied where she had tried to open the hatch to the sail but either it was jammed or she was too weak to open it.

A crusted black bullet hole cratered her right temple where she had taken her life rather than let the disease have it. The rest of her body was unmarked.

A pair of bodies lay near the periscope.

The sub groaned and shuddered as something heavy hit the sail.

Bolan looked up as the ceiling thumped and clacked. "I think they just attached the docking collar to the sail. I'm going up the ladder."

A metallic rapping came back, signaling the docking was complete.

Bolan heaved himself against the wheel. The crash had jammed the hatch and it took long moments of strain before it suddenly spun. Bolan nearly toppled from the ladder with the released effort. He pushed up the heavy hatch and breathed in the fresh air that poured down in a rush. Bolan was staring up the short tube of a submersible rescue docking collar. The tube was sealed to the Korean sub by a massive magnetic ring. Seawater dripped down the sides.

Gary Manning grinned down from the hatch in the recovery vehicle above. "Hey sailor, want a date?"

"It's good to see you." Bolan enjoyed the canned air coming down from the submersible. "It got a little hairy down here."

"Any other survivors?" Manning asked.

"Just me and Dani."

"How's she doing?"

Bolan shook his head. "We really weren't expecting to get rescued."

"Jack got on the horn and confirmed sighting the submarine. That got the U.S. and Canadian military brass in gear. I swam to the island and confirmed you and Sergeant Antonetti had boarded the sub, and I told them that knowing you, you'd either force it to the surface or sink it. A submersible recovery vehicle was loaded into a C-5 in Seattle and flown it all the way to Borden Island."

"How'd you find us?"

"Well, as you can guess, both Canada and the U.S. had naval patrol planes combing the Arctic within hours. Then, surprisingly, right here off the coast of Borden Island, pretty much right above where you are now, they found Lorenzo Renoir floating on the surface like a marking buoy."

"How's he doing?"

Manning rolled his eyes. "It appears he strapped on scuba gear, opened the swimmer delivery chamber and went for a swim. You're at six hundred feet, Mack. The minute the door opened he was crushed like a bug and as he shot to the surface he decompressed, violently. By the time he hit the surface nothing was holding him together but his wet suit, and everything inside of that was sausage. After we found Renoir, we found this tub pretty quickly."

Bolan nodded. "Is there really a vaccine?"

Manning snorted. "What do I know? It's all above my pay grade." He called back into the submersible. "Doc?"

Dr. Ferentinos's bearded face appeared smiling over Manning's shoulder. "Well good morning, Mr. Cooper!"

"Good morning, Nikos. How are you doing?"

"Oh, it's all been very exciting. Getting shot, fighting the Union Corse, North Korean secret submarines, riding around in submersible recovery vehicles at the bottom of the Arctic Ocean." Ferentinos laughed. "You know I normally spend my afternoons peering into petri dishes."

"Speaking of petri dishes…"

"I've cured it." Ferentinos held up a pair of syringes triumphantly. "I can kill the bacteria dead in the bloodstream. As an epidemic, Mutant Pyogenes A is dead issue, but whatever tissue damage it's already done to its victims is irreversible without grafts or transplants. You look pretty healthy all things considered, but I suggest you and Sergeant Antonetti get up here and get inoculated immediately."

Bolan dropped down the ladder. "Dani, let's get out of here."

A pair of Navy SEALs dropped down into the bridge. They looked askance at Bolan and Antonetti and swiftly began gathering up the ship's logs. The lights dimmed significantly was they powered up the ship's computers and began downloading information.

The Executioner had bigger concerns, "Dani, how about our heading back to Kugluktuk and you giving me a proper tour of your hometown?"

"It would be my pleasure," the beautiful Mountie replied.

··· James Axler
Outlanders·

The war for control of Earth enters a new dimension…

REFUGE

UNANSWERABLE POWER

The war to free postapocalyptic Earth from the grasp of its oppressors slips into uncharted territory as the fully restored race of the former ruling barons are reborn to fearsome power. Facing a virulent phase of a dangerous conflict and galvanized by forces they have yet to fully understand, the Cerberus rebels prepare to battle an unfathomable enemy as the shifting sands of world domination continue to chart their uncertain destiny…

DEADLY SANCTUARY

As their stronghold becomes vulnerable to attack, an exploratory expedition to an alternate Earth puts Kane and his companions in a strange place of charming Victoriana and dark violence. Here the laws of physics have been transmuted and a global alliance against otherwordly invaders has collapsed. Kane, Brigid, Grant and Domi are separated and tossed into the alienated factions of a deceptively deadly world; one from which there may be no return.

Available at your favorite retailer.

GOLD EAGLE®

GOUT36

TAKE 'EM FREE
2 action-packed novels plus a mystery bonus

NO RISK
NO OBLIGATION TO BUY

DEATH LANDS®

Atlantis Reprise

GRIM UNITY

In the forested coastal region of the eastern seaboard, near the Pine Barrens of what was New Jersey, Ryan and his companions encounter a group of rebels. Having broken away from the strange, isolated community known as Atlantis, and led by the obscene and paranoid Odyssey, this small group desires to live in peace. But in a chill or be-chilled world, freedom can only be won by spilled blood. Ryan and company are willing to come to the aid of these freedom fighters, ready to wage a war against the twisted tyranny that permeates Deathlands.

In the Deathlands, even the fittest may not survive.

Available December 2005 at your favorite retailer.